MANUSCRIPTS, MEOWS & MURDER

A Dickens & Christie Mystery

Book XI

Kathy Manos Penn

Contents

CHAPTER ONE

DAVE GLANCED MY WAY as he put the car in reverse. "What are you all smiles about this morning? Our trip, I hope."

Studying him from behind my sunglasses, I considered how my life had changed in the two years we'd known each other. It had never occurred to me that our chance meeting at the Olde Mill Inn would turn into a dinner date, much less a transatlantic relationship.

I was a widow of eighteen months when we met, and dating was something I'd yet to consider. Yes, I'd picked up and moved from Atlanta to the Cotswolds—a decision that shocked my family and friends, but I hadn't thought beyond the move.

Perhaps it had been a rash step, but finding and decorating my cottage and making friends in the village kept me busy and helped to keep the tears at bay. I still missed my husband of twenty years, but building a new life in a new place was the jolt I needed. At least, that's the way I saw it. Henry would always be a part of my life, but the sad times slowly gave way to moments of joy. And Dave played a huge role in that.

"Earth to Leta," he said.

Holding my left hand up to the windshield, I felt my face break into a grin. "I'm smiling about this and so much more." My engagement ring sparkled in the sunlight. "Did you ever envision your life like this? Leaving New York City, a swoonworthy proposal, and planning a wedding?"

It was his turn to grin. "Is that how you describe my marriage proposal?" He chuckled. "All that matters is that it worked."

"Did you ever doubt I'd say yes?"

"Let's just say I wasn't leaving anything to chance. I don't think lightning strikes twice, and falling in love with a beautiful, talented woman who loved me back seemed too good to be true."

I blushed. "I'm sure it was Dickens and Christie that clinched the deal, right?"

"Oh yes, acquiring a menagerie was a bonus."

"What's a menagerie?" barked Dickens.

"Seriously? Doesn't he know he belongs to us, not the other way around?" meowed Christie.

Dave looked in the rearview mirror. "What's with the sudden racket back there, you two?"

"I think they took exception to the word 'acquire.' They like to think you're marrying me and adopting them."

I knew he thought I was being playful. He had no clue that I understood Dickens and Christie, and that the three of us regularly conversed. Keeping my strange talent a secret from him was getting more and more difficult.

Whenever I pictured myself telling Dave that I was a female version of Dr. Dolittle, I heard Shakespeare's line, "The course of true love never did run smooth." I'd yet to reveal my secret to anyone, and I didn't see a reason to start now.

We lapsed into our usual companionable silence as we embarked on our trip to Port Isaac. Under any other circumstances, an excursion to Cornwall would be right up my alley. Instead, I was anxious rather than eager.

Months ago, Claire Harris, Dave's editor, had invited him to speak at a writers' workshop she was hosting. We agreed to spend two nights at the workshop and then leave to explore more of Cornwall. With a wedding in our future, we made plans to check out possible wedding venues too. Mousehole, St. Michaels, and St. Mawes were on the itinerary, plus a stop in Truro for dinner with our friend Jake Nancarrow.

All of that changed when Claire called to say she had a last-minute cancellation and invited me as a participant. My first inclination was to say thanks, but no thanks. Sure, Wendy and I had proclaimed we would try our hands at writing a cozy mystery, but since then, very little writing had occurred. Wendy had written what I dubbed a quasi-outline, and I'd done next to nothing. A notebook of scribbled ideas didn't count in my mind.

We had no lack of material, given our penchant for sticking our noses into murder cases, but there was no guarantee that real-life investigating would translate into captivating writing. If that were the norm, bookstores would be overflowing with bestsellers authored by every Tom, Dick, and Harry—or every constable, DI, and DCI. Since I'd yet to write word one in this endeavor, I didn't relish the idea of spending a week sharing my first attempts with critique partners and the Writer in Residence, Issa Wright.

Dave interrupted my train of thought. "If I'm not mistaken, there's a little black cloud hovering over your head. What's up?"

"I'm waiting for inspiration to hit. Why is it that I have no problem writing a newspaper column, but I have no clue how to start *The Canine Caper*? Do I use first person or third? Do I open with a description of the village or a line of dialogue or background on Constable James? Wendy and I have read an unbelievable number of conflicting opinions on how best to hook your reader."

He gave me a bemused look. "That's the benefit of this week, sweetheart. The schedule includes one-hour sessions on dialogue, setting, and more. You can try a variety of approaches and get feedback from one of your favorite writers and from the other participants, not to mention Claire. Then you'll have everything you need to crank out the first book."

"I know you're right. I just hate being so obviously clueless."

"But you're not. You've already got the plot because *The Canine Caper* is based on what happened when Dickens disappeared. You've settled on Jonas as your series lead, with you and Wendy as the meddling amateur sleuths. Writers are told to write what they know, and that's what you're doing. You're a writer, Leta. You're just switching from nonfiction to fiction. Dare I say, piece of cake?"

"Only at your peril. But I know you're right. And it helps that I'm a grammar geek and a word nerd. I have all that going for me, though I'm not infallible. Still, it irks me no end when I read books sprinkled with poor grammar and malapropisms."

That last bit earned me a sidelong glance. "Now, you're just showing off. The others at the workshop may know what a malapropism is, but I doubt many of them have read Richard Sheridan's play, much less taught it."

In my best British accent, I channeled Mrs. Malaprop. "Here's one. 'Illiterate him, I say, quite from your memory.' Illiterate, obliterate, it was all the same to her."

Dave couldn't help himself. "Remember when she describes someone as the 'pineapple of politeness?' That may be my favorite. Maybe you can have a minor character in your book who's prone to misspeaking."

"Not a bad idea. I bet Claire would get a kick out of literary references in the story. It was kind of her to say she'd edit our book, and we certainly don't want to disappoint her."

When we made a brief stop for lunch, we scanned the workshop flyer we'd downloaded. It included not only the schedule but also background on the surrounding area and the towns we'd be visiting on our literary field trips.

When I saw the gleam in Dave's eye, I knew something had struck his fancy. "We've got to try this kayaking tour. It's a great way to see the coastline, and they even visit sea caves when the tide is right."

I shuddered. "As long as I don't have to go inside a cave, I'm game. I don't consider myself claustrophobic, but caves aren't my thing. The schedule allows plenty of free time for writing or exploring, so I'm sure we can squeeze it in."

We arrived in the village of Port Isaac with time to spare. The Clifftop Retreat, our home for the week, was only a short distance farther.

A colorful banner stretched across the tops of the stone columns fronting the entrance. I read aloud, "Welcome to the Pen & Prose Writers' Workshop." Beneath those words, I saw the logos for Harris House and Wyndham Press, the newest imprint for the family-run publishing firm. Claire was our host for the week, and I wondered whether anyone else from the family would make an appearance.

Lined with hawthorn hedgerows, the long gravel drive stretched ahead of us, with an occasional golden beech tree towering above the border. The drive gave way to a courtyard and a large two-story building of grey stone with a slate roof. Smaller grey stone structures flanked it. The red berries on the rowan trees scattered among the buildings provided a touch of color to the fairy-tale setting.

I was so struck by the postcard scene that it took me a moment to notice the blue of the Atlantic beyond the buildings. "Oh my goodness, Dave, have you ever seen such a picturesque setting? I wonder if they're set up to do weddings. We must ask."

"Picturing a cliffside ceremony, are you? I don't imagine you plan to wear a veil, but the wind could wreak havoc with your hair."

I gave him a demure look. "You're quite right. The days of me looking like a blushing bride are long gone. I haven't settled on a look yet, though I'm leaning toward something vintage in cream lace. I'll have to ask Ellie whether a bride can wear a fascinator. You know how I adore hats." Ellie, the Dowager Countess of Stow, was my go-to for etiquette questions.

As I let Dickens out of the car, an elderly man emerged from a nearby cottage. He yelled something over his shoulder and slammed the door. His stature and his thick mane of white hair brought Leonard Bernstein to mind—a surly Leonard Bernstein.

He pulled up short and pointed at me and Dickens. "Don't tell me you've brought a dog! What is it with Brits and their dogs? One can't go anywhere without encountering mongrels." He spoke with a Boston accent.

How dare he?! "I'm not a Brit and Dickens isn't a mongrel. He's a Great Pyrenees, I'll have you know."

Dave pulled Christie's backpack from his side of the car and peered over the roof. "How do you feel about cats? We've got one of those, too."

The man opened his mouth but must have thought better of saying anything more. Instead, he turned on his heel and strode toward the gap in the short, stacked stone fence that extended beyond the cottages. I hoped he was heading to the cliff to blow off steam or yell into the wind or whatever it would take to make him more pleasant.

Removing our bags from the trunk, Dave slammed the lid

down. "Just great. The inimitable Trevor Tarkington is in rare form."

My mouth dropped open. "The man you're on the panel with? Why would Claire pair you with him?"

"Because my original partner had emergency surgery a month ago and Tarkington was already planning to be here with his wife. The behavior you just witnessed mirrors the tone of his book reviews, so Claire came up with the idea to showcase two diametrically opposed approaches to writing reviews. Think of the *60 Minutes* 'Point-Counterpoint' segment in the '70s where Shana Alexander and James Kilpatrick debated the political moments of the day."

"Which writer is his wife?"

Dave grimaced. "It's not just any writer. It's Issa Wright, the Writer in Residence."

"But her writing is so beautiful, so calm and insightful. How can she be married to that—to that ogre?"

"You're not the first person to ask that question. My mother is a saint."

Spinning around, I saw a man petting Dickens. He looked at me and stood with his hand out. "Brax Tarkington, the ogre's son. And by the way, I like dogs."

"Oh my gosh. I can't believe I made that awful comment. I'm so sorry."

The corners of his mouth quirked up. "No worries. Believe me, it's far from the worst thing he's been called. You should read his mail."

Speechless, I looked from him to Dickens and back. He was tall with broad shoulders like his father, but slimmer, and looked to be in his forties. His attire was casual, jeans topped with a brown sweater over a button-down shirt.

He ruffled Dickens's ears. "What's his name?"

"Dickens, and I'm Leta Parker."

"Well, Dickens, don't worry about my dad. His bark is worse than his bite. And he's usually much more polite, at least to women. You just caught him at a bad moment. When I see you next, I'll have Mom in tow, and I'll introduce the two of you."

I stood in stunned silence as he sauntered off. As if I wasn't anxious enough about the week ahead, I'd already stuck my foot in my mouth.

CHAPTER TWO

DICKENS AND I JOINED Dave inside at the front desk, to the left of the large double doors. As he introduced us to George and Charlie, the father and daughter who owned the Clifftop Retreat, a large, long-haired cat wandered our way.

"Look, Dave. Is it a Maine Coon?"

Charlie's eyes twinkled. "You Yanks always ask that. Hagrid is a European Coon, similar to yours, but with slightly different features." She pointed out his elongated ears and square muzzle. "Both are descended from the Norwegian Forest cat, but our version looks more like a creature from the wild."

Both Dickens and Christie commented on Hagrid's size before Dickens took things into his own paws and head-butted the enormous cat. When the two scampered behind the front desk, Charlie gave them treats.

To the right, across the foyer, was a sitting area with a stacked stone fireplace. The entire area was open to the second story with exposed wooden beams. A wide hall extended to the back of the building where a patio with Adirondack chairs was visible. Beyond that was an expanse of green lawn and the ocean. As I stood mesmerized by the view, two windblown women discarded their blankets outside in a large chest and bustled through the glass doors.

Laughing and chatting, they pulled their jackets tight and took turns pouring steaming drinks from the urn at the back of the hall. When Dickens barked a greeting, they looked our way.

"Hello there," called the taller of the two. "We're chilled to the bone. Are you just arriving?"

Dickens took her words as an invitation to run their way and skid to a stop at their feet. "Leta, look, new friends."

Both women set their mugs on the table and knelt to pet him. I caught the words, "Look at you. Aren't you adorable?" as they petted him.

Followed by Dave and Christie, I joined the group. "Hi. I'm Leta Parker and that's Dickens."

The short, curly-haired woman held out her hand. "We two are your romance writer contingent. I'm Evie Pembroke, and this is my friend, Nora Carroway."

Nora stood. "Pleased to meet you and your pup. Wait. Is that a cat in a backpack?"

Dave glanced over his shoulder. "It sure is. This is Christie, and I'm her servant, Dave Prentiss."

"He's finally catching on," meowed Christie.

"Well, I never," said Nora.

Evie squinted at Dave. "You're on the panel tonight, aren't you? I recognize your name. And according to your bio, you must be a J. M. Barrie fan. I somehow missed your article about the children's book he wrote. I'll have to find it."

"You'll easily locate it on the internet. The *Strand* published it, and plenty of other media outlets picked it up. The woman who owns the only copy of the book is a great friend of ours."

Nora was still cooing over Christie but looked my way for a moment. "And you, Leta, are you a writer, or did I miss your name as a presenter?"

"Goodness no. I'm not a presenter, and I'm hard-pressed to call myself a writer, since I haven't yet started the book I'm supposed to be writing. Hopefully, this week will get me going."

That was Dave's cue to put his arm around my shoulder. "Ladies, she's been writing columns for years. She'll be cranking out her first cozy mystery in no time."

Evie clapped her hands. "Marvelous. Can't wait to hear more about it."

Our next stop was our home away from home for the week. As Dave unlocked the door to our cottage, I admired the pumpkins lining the path and pansies and chrysanthemums in the two window boxes. The cottages were named for local trees, and the wooden sign on ours read Ash. Inside to the left, a pottery jug of mums greeted us on the kitchen table, and to the right, a fire burned in the wood-burning stove in the sitting room.

Dave dropped our luggage and turned from side to side. "Wow. Charlie said she'd send someone to light the fire, but I didn't expect it to be done so quickly. Let's stow our bags in the bedroom and relax."

"Let me take Christie. She's probably eager to stretch her legs." When I removed the backpack from Dave's shoulders and lifted her out, she darted straight to the glowing stove. "Guess I was wrong. What she wants is to snooze in a warm spot. Not a bad idea."

A short hall led to the rear of the cottage, where a door opened to the outside. "Look, Dave, we have our own Adirondack chairs and a view of the ocean."

He pointed to the right beyond the neighboring cottages, where we could see the patio behind the main house. "There's a firepit in the middle. It's the perfect setting for a workshop and maybe a wedding, depending on the season."

Our bedroom was off the hall and wasn't large, but the burgundy and green comforter and matching curtains made it look snug and inviting. The room had all the essentials—reading lights, USB ports, a dresser with a mirror, and a chest with extra blankets.

In the bathroom, the vanity was large enough to accommodate my makeup bag and Dave's dopp kit. The only thing missing was a full-length mirror.

"Hmmm. How will you survive a week here, Leta, if you can't see yourself from head to toe?"

"Very funny, Dave. It will be difficult, but I'll manage somehow."

He laughed as I claimed the bottom two drawers of the dresser. "You're such a creature of habit. You always leave me the top drawers, and you have to unpack before you can relax."

"That's me—work before play. And it makes sense for you to get the top drawers because you're tall." I shook out a few items and hung them in the closet and carried my makeup to the bathroom. "Voilà. Now, I'm ready to relax."

Dave was standing in front of the refrigerator. "Look at this, a tray of cheese and crackers. And there's a bottle of red wine on the counter. Shall I open it?"

"I think not. I'm already sleepy, and cocktails are at six. I want to be wide awake and at my best to meet everyone. What about you? Do you need to prepare for the panel discussion?"

"Nope. I've explained my review process before, and what I have to say rarely varies. I've heard Tarkington present, and I've read his reviews, so I have a decent idea of what he'll say. There's no doubt we'll disagree with each other, and we'll give everyone the opportunity to see both sides of the coin. I haven't met Spike O'Malley, the journalist who will be posing the questions, but he sent me the list, and there's nothing unusual about them. I also read several of his articles, and I like his writing."

We spread out on the couch. Dave took one end with his feet on the ottoman, and I stretched out with my head in his lap. To me, napping was one of the best parts of retirement, and I indulged as often as possible. Dave rarely did. I knew he'd be perusing his email and maybe mapping out a day in Boscastle as I snoozed. He had an idea for a book about Thomas Hardy, and the author had lived there with his first wife.

Dave woke me with a kiss on the cheek. "Time to get up, sleepyhead. Cocktails are in an hour, and I'm going to take a quick shower."

Yawning, I followed him to the bedroom and studied my reflection in the mirror over the dresser. "I think I'll just fluff and dust—use the blow dryer and reapply my under-eye concealer."

"You know, I've never known anyone else to use that expression. Other people just say freshen up."

"I don't know where I picked it up, but it explains exactly what I do. I fluff my hair, touch up my makeup, and finish by powdering my nose—fluff and dust."

He turned on the shower and stuck his head out of the bathroom door. "And you say you're not a writer."

As I turned my head upside down to use the drier on my hair, I considered using fluff and dust as a catchphrase for my character in the book. I imagined anyone who knew me would immediately realize that I was the model for the woman who lost her dog. Wendy would be easily recognizable too, though she and I hadn't yet come up with names for ourselves. There was something to that "write what you know" advice.

I pulled on my formfitting black cashmere tunic, the one that extended to mid-thigh. Someone younger might have worn it as a dress, but I chose grey leggings and knee-high black boots. A wide black belt and a shimmering red cat pin completed the outfit.

We debated taking Dickens, given Trevor's reaction to him earlier. "It's up to you, Leta. Dogs are welcome everywhere over here, and you rarely leave Dickens behind."

"You know what? You're right. I wouldn't have given it a second thought if not for that man's rude behavior. Dickens, you're with us."

Thankfully, Christie was happy to stay behind on the warm hearth, so there were no plaintive meows as we headed to my first ever night at a writers' workshop.

CHAPTER THREE

THE SHORT WALK TO the main house was a chilly one, and I was glad I'd chosen my warmest outfit and topped it with my red wool car coat. Inside, a fire was roaring in the two-story fireplace.

As Dave took my coat and went to fetch drinks, Dickens sat at full alert by my side, with his tail going a mile a minute. I could tell he was ready to meet and greet. "Not yet," I whispered.

The two romance writers were chatting with Claire at the makeshift bar on the far wall, and Brax Tarkington stood talking with an attractive white-haired woman seated in a wingback chair. Issa Wright was even more striking in person than she was in her photos.

By the large window, her husband Trevor was deep in conversation with a younger man with a head of unruly ebony hair. Trevor wore a tweed sport coat, and the other man wore a short leather jacket. He also sported an earring. I wondered if that was Spike. To me, his look suited the name.

I turned when the front door opened behind me, bringing in a blast of cool air. The gentleman who entered wore a navy overcoat and carried a valise and a computer bag.

Charlie came from behind the front desk to greet him. "You

must be Mr. Sterling. I'm so sorry you got lost. Let me take your bags."

His face broke into a broad smile. "But now I'm found, and all is well. Things will be even better when I have a cocktail in my hand."

After he and Charlie agreed she could show him to his room later, she took his coat and bags. As he snugged his pale blue scarf around his neck, his eyes fell on Dickens. The look on his face told me he liked dogs.

"And what's your name, boy?" Like most people did, he ruffled Dickens's ears and commented about his diminutive size, which got the usual indignant bark from Dickens.

Holding out his hand, he introduced himself. "Oliver Sterling, romance writer. And you? Besides owner of this handsome dog?"

"Leta Parker, soon to be a cozy mystery writer, I hope. And Dickens is a dwarf Great Pyrenees. That's why he's smaller than usual. Did I hear correctly that you got lost?"

"Yes, I often do. I was deep in thought and missed a turn. Went miles out of the way before I realized it. The good news is that I was thinking through a knotty plot point in my latest book, and I worked it out, so the extra miles and late arrival were worth it."

Dave arrived with our wine, and the two exchanged introductions. As they chatted, I counted the people in the room and surmised that one participant was missing. *Dirk Blackthorne*, I thought. He was a thriller writer, and I'd enjoyed several of his books when I was in my Lee Child phase. The hero in Blackthorne's books was more cerebral than the hulking Jack Reacher, but both series were equally entertaining.

When the man in the leather jacket introduced himself to Dave, I was one step closer to knowing who was missing. "Greetings, I'm Spike O'Malley, and you must be Dave Prentiss."

"That I am. And let me introduce my fiancée, Leta Parker."

Dickens gave a soft whine. "What about me?"

"Oh, and let's not forget Dickens. He's a member of the family."

Spike rubbed Dickens's head and leaned toward Dave. "Are you ready for tonight? I should warn you that Tarkington is in rare form, but when is he not?"

That got an eye roll from Dave. "Right. We got a hint of his mood when he called Dickens a mongrel earlier."

As the two conversed, I caught Brax's eye and joined him and his mother. "Good evening, Brax. I'd love that introduction you promised me."

"Certainly. Mom, this is Leta Parker. We met earlier today, after she encountered Dad."

Issa smiled warmly. "Delighted to meet you, Leta. I know when Brax uses the word encounter, that means my husband wasn't at his best. Fortunately, after tonight, he plans to sequester himself in our cottage. He has a deadline to meet for his latest book. Now, tell me a little about yourself and what you'll be working on this week." The family may have lived in Boston, but neither Brax nor Issa had the strong regional accent Trevor had.

"My best friend and I are allegedly co-writing our first cozy mystery. She's a retired English teacher, and I'm a retired banker who briefly taught English. These days, I write columns for fun. We're both avid readers who've never tackled writing, and I'm here this week with the outline she started."

She studied me with her large blue eyes, as though considering her response. "Well then, according to Ray Bradbury, you already have two things going for you. His advice was, 'Just write every day of your life. Read intently. Then see what happens.' I don't know about your friend, but I suspect you're already writing nearly every day as a columnist."

"That's pretty much what my fiancé says. When I make excuses, he likes to remind me I'm already a writer."

She spoke again in her soft, melodious voice. "What you may be missing is the craft of writing—the elements that will make your story readable. We'll touch on the five key elements this week, some in more depth than others."

"And I have every confidence you and Wendy will master those in no time," said Claire over my shoulder.

With a sudden intake of breath, I spun around. "Goodness. You snuck up on me."

"I didn't mean to startle you. I just wanted to be sure you gave Issa the complete picture."

"About what, Claire?"

"About having a series in mind and already having the plot for the first book."

She placed her hand on my arm. "Issa, it's based on a true story. Talk about writing what you know. Leta lived the first book, and she and her partner have solved several serious crimes in real life."

"That's laying it on a bit thick, don't you think? I'm a novice, plain and simple."

The next person to chime in was Dave. "I keep telling her she's selling herself short."

I rolled my eyes. "You already know Claire. Let me introduce the other member of my cheering section, Dave Prentiss."

"Hi, Dave. I didn't get to introduce myself earlier. I'm Brax Tarkington, and I'm sure you recognize my mother, Issa."

"Happy to meet you both. Are you a writer, too, Brax?"

"Oh no. I leave that to my parents. There are enough authors in the family."

With an affectionate smile, Issa reached up to pat Brax's hand. "What he's not telling you is that neither I nor his father could accomplish what we do without Brax managing our lives, especially these days. Brax is my support in more ways than one."

She pointed to the cane leaning against her chair. "In my husband's eyes, I'm still the young, athletic woman he married. Having Brax at my side keeps that illusion alive for Trevor."

I recalled hearing that Issa had Parkinson's disease but couldn't place when she had revealed her diagnosis. The signs weren't obvious, at least to me. I didn't notice any telltale tremors, nor did I pick up any slurring in her speech. *What an inspiring woman*, I thought. *Still writing and brave enough to conduct a writers' workshop, where she'll be on stage for a week.*

When Claire whispered in her ear, the response was a vigorous nod. Issa braced herself on the arms of her chair and rose. In what looked like a practiced move, she grasped her cane while Brax placed his hand on the small of her back. The two women moved to stand in front of the fireplace, and Brax retreated to the side.

"Good evening," Claire called. She waited until the conversation around the room faded before proceeding. "Welcome to the inaugural Pen & Prose Writers' Workshop. I'm Claire Harris, Editor-in-Chief of Harris House, and your host for the week.

"Before I speak to the week's activities, I'd like to introduce our Writer in Residence, Issa Wright." A smattering of soft applause filled the room. "I can't possibly do justice to her illustrious career in a few brief sentences, but it's all there in the bio in your workshop materials."

She cleared her throat. "Issa is renowned for her work in two genres—children's literature and women's fiction. I'm sure that most of us have enjoyed her children's books or read at least one of her novels. I've read every one of her books in both genres. If you missed the middle-grade books she wrote in the seventies, I recommend you pick up a copy or two while you're here. Reading all the volumes in her *Celtic Dreams and Faerie Schemes* was one of the great pleasures of my childhood. I remember being devastated when my mum told me there weren't any more. Ask my friends what gifts I shower their children with, and they'll name Issa's books."

Claire pointed to Evie. "I see you nodding. Have I struck a chord?"

"Goodness, yes. My children and all my nieces and nephews have those books."

Oliver spoke up. "Indeed. It's a guilty pleasure to reread them before I wrap them as gifts."

Claire turned to Issa. "I'm so glad you didn't stop there. Discovering that you had turned to writing adult books was like finding the pot of gold at the end of the rainbow. I didn't realize right away that Issa Wright was I. Wright, and when I did, it made sense. The themes of friendship, family, and connection come alive in all your books."

Pointing to the mantel, Claire named the books that were displayed. The covers of the children's books were as enchanting as I remembered them. Like the others in the room, I'd given those books to lots of children. For toddlers, my go-to gift was always the Spot books by Eric Hill, but once the children were older, it was *Celtic Dreams and Faerie Schemes.*

When Claire finished her opening remarks, she turned the stage over to Issa. "Claire, you more than did my career justice. Thank you. I'd like to elaborate on one thing, and that's my early pen name." She pointed to a corner of the room where her husband stood. "Trevor and I met at a writers' conference when I pitched *Celtic Dreams* to him. He was an established editor. I was a young nobody, ready to throw in the towel after countless rejection letters."

There were some knowing nods around the room. "Later, over drinks, he suggested I use a gender-neutral pen name and try again. You may recall that J. K. Rowling received the same advice about using her given name nearly thirty years later. Publishers didn't believe that boys would read a tale of adventure written by Joanne Rowling. If not for Trevor's advice, I doubt I'd be standing here in front of you today. His guidance was instrumental in my journey, and I'm immensely grateful for it."

She looked toward him, and I was happy to see a genuine smile spread across his face. Perhaps his earlier sullen demeanor was an aberration—but Brax's explanation made it sound like it was more the norm.

"Have any of you experienced a similar bias?" Claire asked.

Spike gave a hearty laugh. "I'm a journalist, not an author, and I expect you know my mum didn't name me Spike. When I got a job offer as a crime reporter, I was told I needed an edgier name. Why they didn't think Seymour would work is beyond me."

After the chuckles died down, Oliver shared his experience. "The first several books I pitched were traditional romances. When I was fortunate enough to find a publisher for one of them, they asked me to change my name to Olivia Spencer. I guess they didn't see me as the next Nicholas Sparks. We came up with another pen name, nothing like my real one." He looked over at Claire. "No offense, but publishers can be an odd lot."

Issa picked back up. "I suspect I should find comfort in hearing that it's not only women who suffer this bias, but it's still disheartening. As for my pen name, does anyone know why I chose I. Wright rather than E. Wright? My family nicknamed me Issa, but my given name is Elizabeth."

The silence made me picture wheels turning in the brains around the room. Dave spoke first. "Issa, I may be on the wrong track, but is it a declarative sentence? If you remove the period after the initial, you can read it as 'I write.' Is that it?"

"Yes, Dave. It was my version of Neil Diamond's 'I am, I said.'

My declaration that I was a writer, no matter what happened. I see it as prophetic because, to this day, I write. The publishing industry has become more accepting, but it still has a long way to go. I'd like to think that today, a woman could submit *Celtic Tales and Faerie Schemes* under her real name, no matter how obviously feminine, and a publisher would accept it."

She held her free hand toward us, palm up. "And that takes me to my hope for the week—that each of you walks away inspired to fight the good fight, whatever that is for you. Perhaps it's improving your craft. Perhaps it's writing a masterpiece or the book that will bring in the most money—those can be two different things, by the way. Or perhaps it's writing the book that you've had in your head for years, not for any monetary reward but for pure joy."

When Brax placed a glass in her right hand, she held it aloft. "Here's to a marvelous week of writing!"

A cozy dining room with starched white tablecloths wasn't the place for Dickens, so we left him by the fireplace. Claire invited us to grab our place cards from a small table by the door and sit wherever we liked. When Dave and I chose a table for four by the windows, Nora joined us. The remaining guests spread out around the room. Spike and Issa sat at one table; Brax and Evie at another; and Trevor, Oliver, and Claire at a third.

Dressed in a starched white shirt and black bowtie, George offered us our choice of red or white wine. Nora lifted her glass of white before taking a sip. "Here's to a productive week."

She closed her eyes and sighed. "Perfect. Now, I must hear all about you two. I see an antique filigree engagement ring, and I'm dying to hear the story behind it."

Glancing at me, Dave opened with the background on his mother's ring. "It's a short story, Nora. It was my mother's, and even before I told her of my plans to propose to Leta, she offered it to me. Mom's not pushy, but that was her subtle way of letting me know she approved."

"How sweet. Who wants to tell me how you met? Your tale could become the plot for my next book. A later in life romance, or friends to lovers, or enemies to lovers. Which variation are you?"

I could feel myself blushing. "It definitely qualifies as a later in life romance, as you can tell from my grey hair. As for the rest, you'll have to decide."

By now, Dave was grinning. "Stop," I said. "I know you're dying to tell her the part where I thought you were a murderer, right? We have to start with Henry, so you'll just have to be patient."

We already had Nora's full attention, but the mention of murder ensured she was all ears. I provided the short version of losing Henry when I was in my fifties, retiring to England, and meeting Dave at a cocktail party. "You take it from there, sweetheart. I can't wait to hear how you describe the evolution of our long-distance relationship."

As I suspected, he had a ball telling her how I thought he was a villain and how many months it took me to admit that I loved him. He gave her the highlights of leaving New York and moving across the pond, but gave short shrift to his unbelievably romantic proposal.

I had to provide the color commentary on the dinner, the candles, and the flowers. "That was a few weeks ago, and here we are."

Nora beamed. "That's a Hallmark movie in the making. I've

written several proposal scenes, but Dave, yours tops them all."

She was explaining that our story fit perfectly into the later in life romance category when we heard a commotion. I looked around in time to see Oliver grasping his throat and choking. He stood with his chair overturned, and Claire was pounding on his back. When he managed to catch his breath, he waved her off and left the room.

When Claire resumed her seat, Trevor turned to the room. "Just a sip of wine gone down the wrong way. No worries."

The expression on Claire's face told me it was more than that. She was one of the calmest people I knew, and not easily flustered. Something was off. I glanced at Dave and could tell he was having the same reaction I was.

It didn't appear that anyone else had picked up on the odd vibe at Claire's table, and the conversation around the room soon resumed. Thankfully, Nora was a chatterbox and didn't notice that my contribution to the conversation was minimal. I was busy puzzling over what had happened at Oliver's table.

George was removing the dinner plates when Charlie emerged from the kitchen with a tall man in a chef's hat. "Let me introduce the person responsible for tonight's dinner, Chef Duncan Trevorrow. During high season, you'll find him at the Coastal Kitchen in Padstow, so we're fortunate to have him with us this week."

We greeted him with an enthusiastic round of applause, and he told us to be sure to let Charlie know of any special culinary requests we had. Based on this first meal, I was sure that any dish he chose would suit me fine.

As we finished our dessert of Cornish Heavy Cake, Claire announced that tonight's panel discussion would be in the room across the hall, complete with coffee, wine, and after-dinner drinks. Dave returned to the front room to get Dickens, and I ducked into the ladies' room. There, I found Evie and Claire with their heads together.

"Yes, I'll find him. Not a problem," said Evie as she turned and left.

Claire took one look at my face and knew. "You sensed it, didn't you? Trevor Tarkington made light of Oliver's choking because he enjoyed it. I thought his harsh reviews were meant to make people think he was a monster, a persona he shed when he wasn't behind his keyboard or hosting his podcast. I was wrong. So wrong."

I wondered what had gone on at their table, but this wasn't the place. "Given his reaction to Dickens earlier, I think you're right. Either he's always in character no matter where he is or he's exactly what we think—a hateful person at heart."

"My worry is that he'll unleash all that on Dave tonight. If anyone can handle him, it will be Dave."

She was right. "Steam may come out of his ears, but he won't lose his temper."

CHAPTER FOUR

THE FLOOR-TO-CEILING BOOKCASES LINING the far wall were the focal point of this room. In front of it sat an antique desk with a colorful Tiffany lamp. My imagination supplied an image of a Victorian lady with a quill pen to complete the picture.

Pecking me on the cheek, Dave left me and Dickens and strode to the table set up by the large picture window. The comfy chairs lining the other walls told me this room usually functioned as the library. Tonight, three rows of folding chairs in the center of the room faced the speakers' table.

I chose a seat at the far end of the middle row, close to the desk, so Dickens could stretch out. It made an excellent vantage point for people watching, one of my favorite pastimes. Brax escorted his mother to a seat near the door before returning with a cup of coffee for her and wine for himself. Issa looked pale, and I wondered if the day was catching up with her.

When Evie and Oliver came in together and took the seats behind me, Dickens stood and put his head on Oliver's knee. I was sure he had picked up on the distress in Oliver's demeanor.

"If he's bothering you, Oliver, I'll get him to lie down."

"Not a bit, Leta. He can be my guardian angel for the

evening."

I gave him a puzzled look. "To guard against what?"

He jerked his head toward the door, where Trevor Tarkington was standing. "That brute. I won't dignify his vile remarks by repeating them. Let's just say that when I mentioned my husband at dinner, he expressed his disdain in no uncertain terms."

Evie leaned forward. "The world is full of homophobes, but you don't expect someone in his position to be so overtly contemptuous. The gall of the man."

Whatever Trevor said must have triggered the choking fit. Was it his habit to go for the jugular? If so, I wondered what he would throw at Dave.

Issa motioned to her husband, and he approached her with an ill-concealed look of irritation. The look turned to a scowl as she cupped her hand to his ear and stretched up to speak to him. She grasped his arm as he tried to pull away, but he flung it off and stomped to the window.

My unease grew as I watched Brax put a comforting arm around his mother. *What else does the evening hold in store?*

Closing the door, Charlie took a seat in the back of the room as Claire quieted us. "Welcome to our first session, 'The Spectrum of Critique: Finding Balance in Book Reviews.' You may question why I chose this topic for a writing workshop. Would anyone care to offer an answer?"

Nora raised her hand. "As a writer who's received her share of one- and two-star reviews, I can guess. It stings something awful no matter how many five-star reviews you get. I suspect you want us to be prepared for the good and the bad. Am I right?"

"Yes, Nora. If you publish a book, you may not ever be reviewed in a magazine or paper, but you will get at least a handful of reviews on Amazon or Goodreads. Some will be positive. Some may be poisonous. I know authors with hundreds of reviews who still get despondent over the one review that trashes their plot, their main character, or their grammar. It's just human nature."

Claire looked around the room. "The key is to learn from your reviews. Are there aspects of your writing you should emphasize because they resonate with readers? Do you hear the same positives over and over? Then run with them.

"It can feel like a blow to the heart when someone denigrates your writing. After your initial emotional reaction, you must determine whether there's any validity to the criticism. If one reader says your main character is smug or wimpy, but fifty others love her, how should you react?"

"When it's one reader," Evie said, "ignore it. If several readers dislike your character, the critique may warrant consideration. It could give me a chance to build my next character differently if I choose."

"Thanks, ladies. That's precisely why I scheduled this topic. Now, let me formally introduce Spike O'Malley, who will lead our discussion tonight. Spike holds a degree in Journalism from the University of Manchester. After graduating, he spent his early years as a crime reporter for *The Manchester Evening News*. Now, at the *Guardian,* he writes feature articles on topics ranging from culture and entertainment to current affairs. He's best known for his insightful interviews with authors, musicians, and filmmakers."

She motioned toward him where he sat in the front row. "Spike, I can't tell you how delighted I am that you found time in your busy schedule to join us tonight."

Giving a half-bow, he moved to the table by the window. "Claire, it's a pleasure to be here. I grew up in the area, and an excuse to visit is always welcome. I'm looking forward to exploring the Spectrum of Critique with two men who are renowned for their book reviews. I've also got some exciting news to share with you."

He motioned toward Issa with a grin. "Your Writer in Residence, Issa Wright, has agreed to allow me to be a fly on the wall this week as she conducts her sessions on writing. Along the way, I also get to interview her about the new book she's working on."

Delighted exclamations filled the room, in stark contrast to Trevor Tarkington's reaction. His mouth dropped open, and his face turned nearly purple. To say he was stunned would be an understatement. More than that, he seemed angry.

After releasing a new book every other year for three decades, Issa had gone five years since her last one. She had implied more than once that there might not be any more. Being allowed to observe and interview Issa would be a feather in Spike's cap, especially since she hadn't granted any interviews since her Parkinson's diagnosis. Her legion of fans would be ecstatic about the news of another book, so why wasn't her husband?

Spike cleared his throat as Claire took her seat. "Let's get started, shall we? As the title of tonight's session indicates, we want to look at the kinds of reviews authors can expect. Not all reviews are created equal. Our speakers both review books for major publications— *The New York Times, The Strand, Harper's,* and more—but their styles represent opposite ends of the spectrum."

Turning toward Dave, Spike provided an overview of his career—from his stint as an investigative reporter to his decades-long tenure writing articles about authors and their books. He highlighted Dave's article on the discovery of a previously unknown J.M. Barrie children's book and his recent nonfiction book, *Barrie and Friends.*

"Let's call Dave our courteous commentator. When he writes a review, he believes in focusing on the strengths of a book. He doesn't shy away from identifying weaknesses, but he doesn't dwell on them. Am I correct in saying that you prefer not to write a review if you can't find anything positive to say?"

"Yes. My perspective is that there are bound to be people who like a book even if I don't. Why should I bias them against it? For example, I'm a Robert B. Parker fan. I don't think the authors who are continuing his series today are anywhere near as good as he was, but I'm still reading the books because I enjoy the characters. There's no need for me to point out they're not as well plotted."

His lips curled in a faint derisive smirk, Trevor crossed his arms as Spike introduced him. "On the other end of the spectrum, we have Trevor Tarkington, with a different career trajectory and different approach."

He noted Trevor's degree in English versus Dave's in Journalism, and his early years as an editor at a publishing house versus Dave's in investigative reporting. Trevor was the author of the Dallas Steele Mysteries—a twenty-four book series about a private investigator in Texas. The twenty-fifth book was due out in early January.

"Let's call Trevor our contentious critic. He takes an aggressive stance, homing in on weaknesses in the books he reviews. This is evident in his written reviews and on his podcast, 'Tarkington Talks Books'. I don't think I'm overstating when I say Trevor's reviews take a sharp and confrontational tone. Would you agree, Trevor?"

"Yes! Far too many people write namby-pamby reviews that don't tell prospective readers anything useful. I aim to be direct."

Talk about confrontational. Trevor had just drawn a line in the sand.

Spike kicked off with what I termed softball questions, asking each man their preferred genres as readers and who their

favorite authors were. As I expected from Trevor, he commented that Dave's author choices—Robert B. Parker and Robert
Crais—were lightweights. According to him, neither could hold
a candle to Dashiell Hammett or Raymond Chandler, his fa-
vorites. Dave's response was that he liked Trevor's choices but
preferred the characters of Spenser and Elvis Cole because they
were more three-dimensional.

From there, Spike upped the ante by asking which genres
they didn't read. Trevor scorned Golden Age mysteries as stuffy
and made a gagging motion about romance novels. He much
preferred thrillers—both psychological serial killer types and ac-
tion-packed series like the Lucas Davenport books. When Spike
followed up by asking him what he thought of Louise Penny,
he rolled his eyes. "I can tolerate her books to a point. I admire
the twisted minds of her killers, but all that soul-searching by
Gamache? Spare me."

"Interesting," said Dave. "Leta turned me on to Louise Penny,
and what I like about Gamache is exactly what you detest. The
two genres I steer away from are science fiction and fantasy,
though again, Leta gave me a Jodi Taylor book, and now I'm
hooked on her series. It combines time travel, history, and humor."

That got an elaborate eye roll from Trevor. It occurred to me
that the only comment Trevor hadn't pounced on was Dave's
mention of World War II historical fiction as one of his preferred
genres. Perhaps Trevor felt he'd be skating on thin ice if he dis-
dained anything World War II related.

Spike continued with likes and dislikes. "As writers who review books, we don't always have a choice about what we read
professionally, but when it comes to reading for pleasure, how
do you decide? Setting aside genre, are their topics or types of
characters you're drawn to? Conversely, are there those that are

anathema to you?" He motioned to Trevor.

"Give me action in a big city any time. Murder and mayhem, serial killers, police procedurals with no-nonsense detectives—I can read them all day. As long as they don't get carried away with the psychological makeup of the characters."

"And what do you avoid at all costs?"

Trevor pounded the table. "Plots that involve emotional baggage. Characters who moan about their lives or worse—commit suicide. I don't want to read about someone who doesn't see life as worth living. I had to review *The Virgin Suicides,* and it was all I could do to finish it. What a waste!"

When his fist hit the table, several of us in the audience jumped. Both Spike and Dave flinched, and Spike seemed momentarily at a loss for words. As Trevor glanced from Dave to Spike, he looked oddly pleased with their reactions.

Dave jumped in. "What do I like? An engrossing literary mystery. A. S. Byatt's *Possession* and Charlie Lovett's *The Bookman's Tale* are two I particularly enjoyed. Or a well-woven tale set in a bookstore, like *The Storied Life of A. J. Fikry.* Don't get me wrong, I like detective novels and such—but I got tired of serial killers and sexual predators a while back."

I wondered whether Spike had known ahead of time how stark the contrast would be between his speakers. Had he realized they would differ in more than their approach to reviews?

Spike asked each man to expound on why they approached their reviews as they did. No matter the disparaging facial expressions Trevor wore when Dave spoke, Dave refrained from responding in kind. It wasn't until Spike asked what the two did in their leisure time that the tone changed. It didn't surprise me to hear Trevor tick off motorcycling, big game fishing, and hunting. To me, those pastimes fit with his aggressive personality.

When Dave listed running, monthly book club meetings,

travel, and his newfound passion for gardening, Trevor erupted. "Are you telling me you joined a book club? Why? I can't see them reading detective fiction, so what do you get out of it?"

Before Dave could answer him, Trevor pointed to me. "Oh wait. You go because your girlfriend wants you to, right? Anything to keep the little lady happy. That's a hell of a way to make your reading choices."

The audience gasped, but my focus was on Dave. He jerked back as his eyes widened.

Before he could say anything, Spike interjected. "Whoa, Trevor, this is a discussion, not a cage fight—"

Trevor spoke over him. "I should have known, Dave. Lucky for her you're a milquetoast both professionally and personally. Sounds like she has you well trained."

My mouth dropped open as Dickens growled. How would Dave respond? A look of shock flashed across his face, rapidly replaced by one of anger. I sensed we were all waiting for him to either storm out or strike out. Which would it be?

He chose a different option. "It's okay, Spike. Let's pursue this angle and see where it goes."

Putting his arm across the back of his chair, he turned to Trevor. "I'll thank you to leave my fiancée out of this, Tarkington. Now, as far as our book club is concerned, it's introduced me to at least one genre I never would have picked up. Do you read women's fiction?"

"Hell no!"

"It isn't something I would have chosen, either, but our book club selected one of Issa's earlier novels—*Summer Solstice*—for August. As you must know, she's a masterful writer. The setting, the relationships, the dialogue—I couldn't put it down."

Dave waited a beat. "Now tell me, do you read *your wife's* books?

Trevor stared mutely at Issa.

There was a lengthy silence until she filled it. "Are you going to answer the man, Trevor? Or shall I?"

Trevor rubbed the side of his face. "That . . . that was the last one I read."

Issa Wright was an award-winning author who had written several novels after *Summer Solstice*. Why had Trevor stopped reading his wife's books?

His astonishing admission brought the evening to an awkward close. Issa struggling to her feet with Brax's help seemed to spur Spike to a decision. He jumped to his feet and thanked both men for an enlightening discussion, asked for a round of applause, and beckoned to Claire.

I could only hope that Issa was right when she said we wouldn't see much of her husband after tonight. I didn't relish the idea of encountering the man again.

CHAPTER FIVE

As OLIVER, EVIE, AND Nora crowded around Spike and Dave, Claire gave me a questioning look and pointed to the drinks table. Dickens and I joined her there.

She picked up a bottle of Irish whiskey. "I didn't know Dave drank whiskey, but this is what he requested, and Spike asked for the same."

"It's rare he drinks hard liquor, but I can see why he would tonight. Here, I'll take it to them, and then let's you and I continue with wine by the fireplace."

Standing behind the two men, I placed a glass of whiskey in front of each of them and whispered in Dave's ear. "You know you held your own, right?"

He pecked me on the cheek. "How obvious was it that I wanted to leap across the table and throttle him?"

Oliver piped up. "For a moment, I thought you would, but you did a masterful job of restraining yourself."

Taking a slug of whiskey, Dave clenched his fists. "If he says another word about Leta, all bets are off." He shook himself and touched my hand. "I need to take the edge off, may even take a walk. Don't wait up for me, sweetheart."

In front of the fireplace, Claire seemed lost in thought. She turned as Dickens ran to her side. "Thank goodness that's over. If I'd had any inkling how horrid Trevor Tarkington could be, I would have eliminated the panel discussion altogether. Dave could have shared his philosophy on writing reviews and given us pointers about what he looks for."

"The road to hell is paved with good intentions. With someone less argumentative, it would have been an enlightening discussion."

A crooked smile appeared on Claire's face. "If I think about it, it was quite enlightening, just not in the way I planned. Not only are the authors prepared for the worst in a review, they now know more about Trevor Tarkington than they ever wanted to. He revealed his true colors tonight."

"The person I feel sorry for is Issa. How did she write her uplifting books while living with him?"

"Maybe," said Claire, "her books were a way to escape her life. The main character in each of them endures emotional turmoil and finds happiness in the end. I need to go back and look at the men in her books. I wonder whether any of them are modeled after her husband."

I was too keyed up to sleep, so I fired up my laptop and took a stab at writing the opening scene of *The Canine Caper*. I chuckled to myself as the words, "It was a dark and stormy night," entered my brain. I'd have to do better than that.

Wendy had suggested writing it in first person in Constable James's voice. After struggling for an hour, I shifted to third person. The words flowed a bit better but were still a struggle.

I sent it off to Wendy for feedback and let Dickens out. As I waited for him to return, Christie joined me outside. "Where's Dave?"

"Tying one on, I think."

"With a rope?"

I chuckled and explained the idiom to my curious cat. She trotted toward the main house, meowing, "This, I have to see."

When she ignored my call to come back, I decided she'd be safe enough until Dave arrived to let her in. At least Dickens and I would get a full night's sleep.

Christie woke me with her sandpaper tongue. "They're both snoring," she meowed. When I put my feet on the floor, Dickens stirred and rolled over, but Dave never moved.

Only after I showered and dressed did he utter his first words. "Aspirin. Do you have aspirin?"

"So, it was that kind of night, was it? Do you want coffee too?"

His only response was a groan. I left him in bed with a warm cloth on his head, water on the nightstand, and Christie tucked against his side. It looked like Dickens and I were on our own, at least until lunch.

The sun was rising as we made our way to breakfast. I was telling Dickens he'd have to wait by the fireplace when Charlie called my name. "Leta, you can take him to the dining room. Plenty of guests do that."

"Hi, Charlie. It's something about the white tablecloths that makes me hesitate to let him join me."

She brushed away my explanation. When Oliver approached from the hall and echoed her sentiment, that was that. "Come on, Dickens. You're now our official mascot."

We two, or we three, were the first ones there. Scrambled eggs, beans, and toast—all the fixings for a traditional English breakfast awaited us. With our plates heaping, we dug in.

Oliver slipped a bite of bacon to Dickens. "I enjoyed Dave's presentation last night. Is he joining us today?"

"Not this morning, but he'll take in a few sessions this week when he's not exploring the countryside. He has an idea for a second book and wants to do some research."

As we ate, the others drifted in. Nora stopped by to say good morning, and I excused myself. "Dickens and I need to get in a walk before this morning's session. See you in the library at nine."

We went out through the patio door and walked toward the cliffs. Dickens held his head high, taking in the smells from the sea and the woods. A low two-rail fence was visible in the distance along the cliff top. As we neared the edge, I saw motion detector lights scattered between the fence posts, though the sunlight filtering through the clouds was enough to keep them from popping on. "The lights are a smart idea, Dickens. On a dark, moonless night, this could be a dangerous spot."

Turning to the right, I ambled along the path as Dickens scampered ahead. We passed a worn wooden bench that had seen better days. The tide was in, and waves were crashing against the rocks below. Up ahead was a small wooden platform with a railing. If Dickens hadn't stopped, I would have missed the path that angled down from it to the left. Stone steps cut into the cliff side formed a steep narrow path to the beach, and I envisioned a young couple carrying a picnic basket on a warm day or an athlete setting out for a run—mindful of the tide tables, of course.

"Time to get back, Dickens. Are you ready for class, or would you prefer to stay with Dave?"

"I'm with you, Leta. I like your new friends."

I went straight to the wood-burning stove in the library to warm my hands. Tomorrow, I would have to remember my gloves. As I shed my jacket and looked for a seat, I noticed a man in one of the wingback chairs along the back wall.

"Oh, hello. I didn't see you sitting there. You must be Dirk Blackthorne. I'm Leta Parker and this is Dickens."

With his salt and pepper goatee, he reminded me of my innkeeper friend Gavin, except that, unlike Gavin, he had striking blue eyes. He chuckled. "I thought so. The dog was a dead giveaway."

At my puzzled look, he explained. "I met Dave last night, and he told me all about you, the dog, and the black cat. Is the cat joining us today, too?"

"You never know. Did you get in late last night?"

"A bit. According to Dave and Spike, I missed an interesting evening."

I rolled my eyes. "That's one way to describe it. My hope is that we don't have a repeat."

When Issa and Brax arrived, she took her place behind the Victorian desk. Brax placed colorful folders in the chairs, which were now positioned facing the desk and the bookshelves. It was Issa's turn on stage.

She looked every bit the lady of the manor, a woman who belonged behind that desk. Her soft white hair was in a chignon, and she wore a lace-edged, high-necked, lavender dress with a cameo pin. Gathered at the wrists, its long sleeves were also edged in lace. *Judy Collins,* I thought. *She's the spitting image of Judy Collins.* I wondered if she ever wore her hair down as the singer did.

Brax closed the door at nine on the dot. There were eight of us—Brax, Issa, Claire, Evie, Nora, Oliver, Dirk, and me. When Spike failed to appear, I wondered whether he was in as bad a shape as Dave. Thankfully, there was no sign of Trevor either.

Since I'd never written a book, much less been in a critique group, I took copious notes on the dos and don'ts. Sharing my work with anyone other than Wendy wasn't something I was looking forward to, but I would do it.

Issa turned us loose at ten to write until noon, when sandwiches would be available in the dining room. With a to-go cup of coffee in my hand and Dickens by my side, I headed to our cottage.

When I opened the door, the empty coffeepot on the counter told me Dave was among the living. Dickens darted into the bedroom while I retrieved my laptop from the sitting room. "Not here, Leta. Wonder where he is."

Christie came yawning from the bedroom. "He left for a run, and he didn't feed me. What's his problem?"

I stopped long enough to put a dab of wet food in her dish. "He has a hangover. The run will either cure him or send him back to bed."

Ensconced in an Adirondack chair, I propped my laptop on my knees and checked my email for a response from Wendy. Her reaction to the first scene was that maybe the series was best written with me as the main character. That was an odd shift. How could we write a series about Constable James if he wasn't telling the story?

Since this week was all about learning, I thought, "Why not?" Starting over, I opened with Lily, a temporary name for my alter ego, being awakened by a cat. The cat's name was Agatha, but she was Christie's doppelganger. To my surprise, the first two paragraphs took shape in no time. It was much easier to tell the story in my voice.

I was putting the finishing touches on the scene where Dickens and his friend Buttercup take off when I heard a shout. Dave was running toward our tiny patio from the cliff.

He was breathing so hard; he could barely get the words out.

"Leta, call 999! There's a body—a body on the rocks."

CHAPTER SIX

As I DIALED, HE yelled he was going back to see if the person was alive. "There's a path to the beach. I'll try to get to him."

I gave the information to the 999 operator—body on the beach, Clifftop Retreat in Port Isaac, not sure if the person's alive or dead, trying to get down there to see.

My brain swirled with questions. Dave referred to the person as him. Who could it be? I hadn't seen Spike, Trevor, George, or the chef this morning. Was it one of them? My next thought was to find someone to help Dave.

Followed by Dickens, I jogged to the back patio of the main house and raced up the hall to the front desk, where Charlie was on the phone. "Leta, what's wrong?"

"Dave needs help. Is your father here?"

She pointed toward the fireplace. "No, he's gone to meet Duncan at the farmer's market, but Brax and Dirk are right here."

They must have sensed my urgency, because they were by my side before I knew it. It was Brax who spoke first. "Leta, what is it? Is Dave sick?"

Breathlessly, I explained the situation. As the three of us raced down the hall to the back door, I yelled to Charlie that I'd already called 999.

Brax reached the fence first. I could see him peer over the edge and glance to the right. "I see Dave, but I don't see anyone else."

He must have spotted Dave taking the path down the cliff. I couldn't hear Dave's response, but Brax jogged in the opposite direction, and I lost sight of him.

By the time Dirk and I made it to the edge and looked over, Dave was running along the rocky beach toward us. When I called his name, he pointed past us. "Down there."

Brax stood motionless farther along the path near the fence, a look of horror on his face. "It's Dad."

Holding onto his arm, I looked down and saw a man sprawled across a boulder. A knit cap covered his head, and he wore a royal blue jacket. "Are you sure, Brax?"

"That's his windbreaker. Who else can it be?"

We watched as Dave scrambled up the boulder. He got close enough to grasp the man's wrist and feel for a pulse. When he looked up and shook his head, we knew we were too late.

Motioning to Dirk, I whispered in his ear. "Can you go back and wait for the police? And for goodness' sake, don't give out any details. We may follow you, or we may wait here. It depends on what Brax wants to do."

As Dirk retraced his steps, I realized there was a wooden bench near the tree line, and I steered Brax in that direction. Wordlessly, he sank onto it and stared at the horizon. I grasped his hand, and Dickens leaned against his legs.

The view was breathtaking, marred only by my knowledge of what lay at the bottom of the cliff. The clouds scudding across the pale blue sky seemed to touch the darker blue of the water below. For the first time, I took in the pockets of bracken along the cliff edge. Most of the large fronds were still dark green, while others had turned the yellow hue common in the fall. When I caught a glint in the sunlight at the cliff's edge, I thought it must be glass.

It was difficult to judge how much time passed, but eventually Brax put his other hand on Dickens's head. "I have to tell Mom, but I don't know how."

A young female officer came toward us, and I couldn't help thinking she looked like a teenager. *They look younger all the time*, I thought. She peered down and shook her head before introducing herself and waiting for us to do the same.

"I'm Leta Parker, and this is Brax Tarkington. We think that's his father down there."

She told us that her partner was taking the path down and would report back shortly. Pulling her aside, I explained that my fiancé had spotted the body and was now waiting down below. Brax spoke not a word.

Her response surprised and relieved me. "We'll secure the area while we wait for DI Nancarrow to arrive."

When she pulled out a notepad, I knew what was coming. "Now, Miss Parker, I understand you called 999. You say your fiancé alerted you. What happened after that?"

Reciting my actions as succinctly as possible, I motioned to Brax. "He thinks it's his father."

Brax looked up. "It's his blue jacket. I know it's him."

"If there's any ID in his pockets, my partner can tell us in a moment." When her mic crackled, she walked up the path. Her grim look as she returned told me that Brax was right.

"Mr. Tarkington, I'm sorry to have to tell you that you're correct."

When there was no reaction, she turned to me. "Is there somewhere private where we can meet with you and Mr. Tarkington? And the other man—Mr. Blackthorne, I think it is?"

By now, the rest of the guests surely knew something was wrong, but not exactly what. They couldn't have missed the police car and ambulance. Until the police notified everyone, I thought our cottage would be the most private spot. Brax and I could go in the back door and hope no one else noticed.

The young constable agreed and spoke into her mic to inform her partner before turning to me. "Go on. We'll catch up as soon as we can. Be a dear and brew a spot of tea, will you?"

If she seemed unbelievably young to me, I, apparently, seemed old to her. *Be a dear! She may as well have called me a doddering old lady.*

"Is it okay for us to tell Brax's mother about this? Or is there some rule that says we can't?"

Her hesitation made me wonder whether the tragic scene was her first experience with something this serious. When she walked away to radio her partner, I felt sure I was right.

She turned back to Brax. "This has to be traumatic for you. Do you feel up to telling your mother or would you prefer to wait for a Family Liaison Officer to help?"

Rubbing his face, Brax gulped. "She'll never forgive me if she finds out I knew and kept it from her."

It was time for me to intervene. "Constable, I've had experience comforting people in these circumstances, and I can help."

Brax reacted as though I'd thrown him a lifeline, and we three agreed I would accompany him to Issa's cottage. The constable would join us there when she could.

I hadn't realized the Tarkingtons' cottage was next to ours, nor that it was larger. "Brax, is this a two- or three-bedroom cottage?"

"It's only two bedrooms, so there was no room for me." He must have seen my surprised look. "Dad was anxious about disturbing Mom. He alternated between being blind to her Parkinson's and treating her like a fragile figurine. Sleeping in separate bedrooms was one by-product."

When Brax knocked on the door, we heard Issa speaking as she approached and opened it. She was on the phone and beckoned us in. "No, Harvey, I haven't seen him this morning. I don't know why he's not answering his phone. You know how he gets. He's probably holed up somewhere with his pad and pen, either a quiet nook or possibly the local pub."

She rolled her eyes at Brax and tried to end the call. "Yes, when I see him, I'll tell him. Bye now."

Slipping the phone in her pocket, she clutched her cane and moved to a chair in the sitting room. "Honestly, the man is incorrigible—your father, not Harvey. He owes him a partial rewrite and is weeks behind. I don't suppose you've seen him, have you?"

Brax straightened his shoulders. "Mom, I don't know how to tell you this, but Dad . . . Dad had an accident. He's . . . he's dead."

"Don't be silly, Brax. Your father's fine. He's off gallivanting, as usual." When there was no response, she leaned toward her son. "Isn't he?"

Taking his mother's hand, Brax shook his head. "No, Mom, he's here, on the beach. He had an accident, and he's dead."

People reacted differently to shocking news. Some burst into tears; some argued; still others were dumbstruck. When Brax repeated the phrase "he's dead," Issa blanched and put her hand to her face. Slowly, she uttered the words, "He can't be. Tell me there's been a mistake."

Shock, anger, rejection, acceptance—those were the stages the bereaved cycled through, as I well knew. Dickens had followed us in, and now he laid his head on her lap. She rubbed his snout as she waited for Brax to answer her.

Ever so gently, he reached his hand to her chin. "Mom, I'm

sorry. There's no mistake. I saw him. The police are here now."

When Issa didn't respond, he moved a footstool to the chair and sat. Looking from his mother to me, he raised his eyebrows and mouthed, "What now?"

Holding up my hand, I walked to the kitchen. Tea bags, sugar, and a kettle were in plain view, as was an empty bottle of Macallan's Scotch. "What we need is tea, and all the fixings are here. Would you like to see to that, Brax, while I sit with your mother?"

He came to my side and whispered, "Thank goodness you're here, Leta. I have no idea what to say, but I know one thing—she needs a doctor. She's one tough cookie, but this news could exacerbate her symptoms. Do you think George or Charlie can find us a doctor?"

"Brax, you don't need to say anything. You just need to be here with her. I'll tell you what. You stay while I find Charlie and work on locating a doctor. Dickens can keep Issa company while you fix the tea—or coffee, if you prefer."

I trotted toward the main house, hoping that Charlie would be at the front desk. When I opened the door, a tantalizing aroma wafted my way, and I wondered if it might be a hearty stew or soup. I'd have to see about having a tray delivered to the Tarkingtons' cottage.

George was back from the farmer's market and was adding logs to the fireplace, and Charlie was on the phone. "George, I need your help and Charlie's, too." He joined me at the desk as Charlie wrapped up her call.

We were alone, but I still pitched my voice low. "I know you're aware of what's going on, but has anyone told you who it is at the bottom of the cliff?"

George shook his head. "We knew from you that there was a body on the beach, and we were hoping against hope the person was still alive. The police asked the quickest way to access the cliff path, and that was it. No one has updated us since. Told us to stay put, if you can believe it."

I debated how much to reveal and concluded, what the heck? Their knowing now or twenty minutes from now wouldn't make a difference to the investigation. "Please don't breathe a word until the police tell you it's okay, but it's Trevor Tarkington on the beach—on a boulder, to be precise—and he's dead."

Charlie was the first to speak. "What happened, Leta? Ever since you ran in here earlier, I wondered if whoever it was got trapped at high tide. Except it's easy to see when the tide's coming in. Do you know what happened?"

Telling them the little I knew didn't take long. "What I need now is a doctor for Issa. Can you contact your local GP and let him know she has Parkinson's? That will tell him what he's dealing with, beyond the obvious."

As Charlie picked up the phone, I asked George if he could deliver lunch to the Tarkington cottage.

"I'll take care of that, and you'll need to eat as well. I'll bring a tray to your cottage, and theirs."

With father and daughter occupied, I had a moment to think. An image had flashed through my brain when Charlie asked her questions, but I'd lost it. Standing in front of the fireplace, I stared into the flames and retraced my steps from the moment I'd heard Dave's shout.

It was something about the fence. I pictured the two rails that spanned the path, what I'd viewed on my morning walk, what I'd seen with Brax and Dirk. That was it! Across from the bench where Brax and I waited, the top rail was broken. Had Trevor leaned against it? Had it given way? Or worse? Had someone helped him to his death?

As if to distract me from my somber thoughts, Hagrid appeared out of nowhere and escorted me to the door. "If you're looking for Christie, she's in the kitchen. She says my food is tastier than hers."

"Of course she found her way to the kitchen. Heaven forbid she go an hour without food."

As I stepped outside, I heard my name and looked up to see DI Jake Nancarrow carrying two suitcases. *Why on earth does he have suitcases?*

He dropped them in front of me and pecked me on the cheek. "Leta, it's not enough that you reported a death. I see you've already called in reinforcements."

"What do you mean, reinforcements? Dave is here, but that's it, unless you mean Dickens and Christie."

Those words were barely out of my mouth when I saw a head of white hair in the distance. "Is that Belle?" And there was Wendy bringing up the rear. I would have expected to see Ellie, too, but I knew she was visiting her villa in Provence.

"What are they doing here? Had I called them the minute Dave made his discovery, there's no way they could've made it here this quickly. It's a four-hour drive to Port Isaac from Astonbury."

"Given the circumstances, I shouldn't be smiling," said Jake, "but they were as shocked to see me as I was to see them."

Bursting with excitement, Wendy greeted me. "Surprise! Dave and Claire invited us. And what a treat to see Jake here, too."

Belle's soft white curls shook as she laughed. "No offense, Jake, but what I'm most excited about is meeting Issa Wright. She's one of my favorite authors."

Wendy put her hands on her hips. "You'd think she'd be more excited about us writing our first mystery, but no. It's all about Issa Wright."

Jake and I exchanged looks. Who would've thought Belle's

favorite author would suffer a sudden real-life tragedy? Whether it turned out to be a tale of an accidental death or something sinister remained to be seen.

CHAPTER SEVEN

JAKE AND I GAVE Belle and Wendy an abbreviated account of what had transpired that morning, and left them to check in. I was ready to dash to the Tarkington cottage, but Jake stopped me. "Hold on. I need the lay of the land before I catch up with my team. I can't believe you're involved with another death at a book festival. Is this a big event like the Poison Pens Literary Festival in Torquay?"

"It's not a festival, and I'm not involved with a death. This is a more intimate event, a writers' workshop with classes interspersed with visits to the homes of famous authors like Daphne du Maurier. We kicked off with a panel discussion last night. Dave was a speaker, as was the dead man. There's only a handful of us who are participants, and we met with Issa Wright this morning and then went off on our own to write."

I paused to catch my breath. "And I didn't find the body. It was Dave."

This was déjà vu. "Oh hell, Jake. It may be a small event, but there's still a schedule for the week. It's like the event in Torquay in that regard, and at one p.m., we're meeting to critique each other's writing. And later, Issa is leading a session on dialogue—at least she was."

"Let me guess. You want me to sort it so you can carry on, right?"

"Yes, I do. Claire will be devastated if we have to cancel. Except I'm not sure how she'll manage without her Writer in Residence."

"I can't help with that, but I don't see a need to halt the workshop if the host wants to go on. If it was an accident, there's no need to cancel. If it wasn't, it will suit my purposes to have everyone remain on the premises. Why don't you tell her not to worry and that I'll speak with her after I visit the scene?"

Jake was fine with me checking on Issa and Brax, so I stopped by the Tarkington cottage. For the first time, I took in the name above the door—Willow. Mother and son held cups of tea that had gone cold, and Dickens was asleep by Issa's feet.

As I brewed a fresh pot of tea, I told them Charlie was fetching a doctor. It didn't surprise me that Brax was relieved while Issa pooh-poohed the idea that she needed one. I thought Brax was right to be cautious. Issa was wan and her voice was weak. Having a doctor check her out couldn't hurt.

"DI Nancarrow is here now, so I expect we'll know more before long." When I explained I was friends with him, I couldn't tell whether they were impressed, relieved, or a mix of both.

Brax took a deep breath. "Mom, he'll want to speak with us, and he'll want to know when you last saw Dad, his mood, and all that."

Issa gave her son a sharp look. "What do you mean, his mood? You're not suggesting this is anything other than an accident, are you?"

While Brax stumbled over his words, I focused on his mention of mood. Given the broken fence, I was sure Trevor had fallen to his death. I glanced at the empty bottle of Macallan's on the counter and wondered how much he'd consumed last night. Was it enough to make him stumble against the fence? Did Brax think his father could have jumped? How likely was it that a man who railed against suicide would take his own life?

As much as I wanted to ask, I stopped myself. I was here to write a mystery, not solve one. Wasn't that what Wendy and I told ourselves in September? That it was time to step away from investigating murders?

I freshened the cups of tea. "George is sending lunch over, and I'm going to check on Dave, unless there's something more I can do."

Issa was quick to respond. "No, Leta, you've done plenty already . . . but, oh no. What about the rest of the workshop? What will Claire do? I would hate for her to cancel it."

Frowning, she closed her eyes. "What am I thinking? Claire can handle the workshops. She knows these things like the back of her hand."

I assured Issa that I would speak with Claire, and I beckoned to Dickens. "Let's go. They don't need you underfoot."

Scratching Dickens beneath his chin, Issa stopped me. "Leta, he's such a comfort. Can he stay with us for a while?" Dickens's wagging tail was all the answer I needed.

Christie was sunning herself on the stone pathway in front of our cottage. "Did you know that Belle and Wendy are here? Hagrid says they have a room in the big building, near the kitchen."

"Next, you'll tell me you want to stay with them to be near the food." Her only response was to lick a paw.

Wendy was the first to greet me when I followed the voices to the patio. "We let you two out of our sight for a day and look what happens. Dave was just giving me his eyewitness account."

I grabbed the remaining bowl of soup and sat on the low stone wall. "Where's your mum?"

"Would you believe she chose to eat in the dining room? I left her explaining to Evie and Nora how we had surprised you. And, yes, she knows not to share anything about the body at the bottom of the cliff. She's playing her innocent little old lady role to the hilt."

"Speaking of surprises, Dave, would you care to tell me how you hatched this plan?"

"It was Claire's idea. I explained how anxious you were about sharing your writing with a group of strangers, and she suggested inviting Wendy. She had another last-minute cancellation and had a spot available. This time it was a fantasy writer and her husband. The poor woman broke her hip."

Wendy leaned forward. "When I told her I was reluctant to leave Mum because Peter's gone to Yorkshire with Lucy, she invited Mum, too. The room and meals are already paid for, so the more the merrier, she said."

The twins were vigilant about not leaving Belle on her own, and Peter rarely traveled. "She even asked if Ellie would want to come, but you know she's in France."

What more can a girl ask for? A fiancé who reads her every mood and a best friend always willing to help. "You two have outdone yourselves, and I'll have to thank Claire, too. I feel less stressed already—about writing, that is. Not about this morning's grim discovery."

"Leta, I'm so glad it worked out. You can't believe how excited Mum is about meeting Issa Wright, and Dave may take her to the Boscastle Visitor Centre to see the flood exhibit. She's also a *Doc Martin* fan, so she's eager to tour Port Isaac. Except, I don't expect she'll get to do all that now."

I caught Dave eyeing the single piece of pie left on the lunch tray. "Not on your life. I'll save you a smidgen, but I get first dibs."

Trading my empty bowl for pie, I forked a small piece. "I asked Jake about continuing the workshop, and he didn't see a problem. Though I haven't spoken with Claire, I bet she'll want to carry on even without Issa. Belle may miss out on spending time with her favorite author, but the rest should work out."

Dave's eyes lit up when I took a second bite and handed him the rest. He'd taken up running, but I still couldn't fathom how he could consume sweets nonstop without gaining an ounce. "Have you filled Wendy in on our experience with Trevor Tarkington?"

"More or less," he said between bites. "I gave her the highlights, but it was difficult for me to recite the entirety of our exchange on the panel. Eventually, I'd like to hear what you remember. This is one of those instances where it's hard not to speak ill of the dead, isn't it?"

"Yes. He must have had some redeeming qualities for Issa to have stayed married to him, but not many were on display last night. She was so gracious about the advice he gave her when they met. What happened to them?"

I could tell from Wendy's expression that I'd lost her. "He admitted last night that he no longer reads her books, and you could tell it was a bone of contention between them. Of course, it was! How could he not read his wife's books?"

Wendy glanced at Dave. "Take that as fair warning. You'll have to read ours."

"That goes without saying. And since you're basing them on the escapades you two have had, there's no telling what I'll learn."

"Let's not forget, Tommy, that you've joined us on several of those so-called escapades. As I recall, we all worked together to clear Claire's fiancé."

"I love it when you two call each other Tommy and Tuppence.

I'm waiting for Dave to get a roadster you can tool around in."

Our conversation came to an abrupt halt when we saw Jake and Claire heading our way from the cliff side. Both wore grim expressions.

Seeing Claire near to tears, I knew the scene on the beach had brought back painful memories for her and wondered whether she'd told Jake about her sister's death.

Jake was in command mode. "Leta, I'll need to interview you and Dave about last night, but first things first. Claire will gather the guests in the library so that I can apprise them of the situation, and you three and Belle should be there too. While Claire's doing that, I'll speak with the Tarkingtons."

I waited for him to say more and bit my tongue when he strode toward Willow Cottage. "Claire, do you know—?"

"He hasn't said. He volunteered that there was no need for me to cancel the workshop but didn't explain. Hopefully, he'll be more forthcoming when we meet in the library. I texted Charlie to spread the word that we're delaying the critique group to hold an impromptu meeting. Everyone knows the police are here, and the sooner we clear the air, the better."

"Will you carry on, Claire? Issa told me she hoped you would. She's confident you can take over her sessions."

She wiped away a tear. "That's so like Issa, always selfless. Yes. Assuming the rest of the writers want to stay, that's my plan. It's a small group, so if several drop out, it will hardly be worth it."

As we followed Claire to the main building, we saw the Scene of Crime Officers departing and the body being transported to the ambulance on a stretcher. I hoped that neither Brax nor Issa were looking out the window. That was a sight they could do without.

Christie trailed behind us and leaped into Belle's lap in the library, where she made biscuits before curling into a purring ball. Dave joined Dirk and Spike, who were deep in conversation by the window. On either side of Belle, Nora and Evie cooed over Christie. Only Oliver sat by himself in the middle of the room.

Steering Wendy that way, I took a seat beside him. "Oliver, you met Belle at lunch, but let me introduce her daughter Wendy. We're working together on the cozy mystery I mentioned."

"Charmed, I'm sure. Unfortunately, you haven't arrived at a very propitious time. Leta, do you know anything? I gather you've spoken with the police."

Jake and Claire walking through the door saved me from having to answer. She appeared unsettled by whatever Jake was saying to her, and they whispered back and forth for what seemed an age. Finally, she nodded in agreement and took her place in front of the desk.

She thanked the group for their patience and introduced Jake. "You're aware that the police have been onsite for several hours, and I know you have questions. Detective Inspector Nancarrow is the senior officer in charge of . . . well, the investigation. He'll explain."

CHAPTER EIGHT

JAKE'S COMMANDING PRESENCE SERVED to quiet the room. "Ladies and gentlemen, I regret to inform you that a tragic incident has occurred here at the inn. Trevor Tarkington died during the night, and we are investigating to determine the circumstances. I understand this news is distressing. For now, I kindly ask for your cooperation and understanding as we proceed with our inquiries.

"I've had a conversation with Miss Harris, and we've agreed that the workshop can proceed as planned. In fact, your presence here will assist our investigation, as you'll be readily available for further questioning as necessary. Additionally, I've personally spoken with Issa Wright and her son Brax, who plan to remain on the premises while the coroner completes her analysis."

His words hung in the air until Oliver raised his hand. "May I ask where he was found?"

"At the bottom of the cliff. I'm not at liberty to divulge details, but I can say that we consider the circumstances suspicious. For that reason, my team will need to interview each of you about your movements last night and in the early hours of the morning."

He motioned to Claire. "Miss Harris will detail the schedule adjustments, and I'd appreciate it if you would provide your cell phone numbers to my constable at the front desk."

Claire took over as Jake stepped aside. "We've delayed the critique group meeting, but we'll hold it next after a brief break, if you all feel up to it. With all the goings-on, you may have forgotten to print and copy your work, but Charlie's standing by to handle that.

"In Issa's place, I'll be leading the classes on characterization, dialogue, setting, and point of view. Are you okay with rescheduling tonight's session to allow time to absorb today's shocking news?"

No one objected to the schedule adjustments, and Evie voiced what most of us were thinking. "Thank you. A critique group is doable. It will be a welcome distraction, but there's no way I'd be able to focus on a class tonight. It's better to process the news and start fresh tomorrow."

"I have one more thing to share. DI Nancarrow has given me the extraordinary news that Issa has asked to carry on with the one-on-one coaching sessions. She's determined to fulfill her commitment to work with you individually. If, for any reason, you're uncomfortable with that arrangement, please let me know."

Jogging to Ash Cottage, I opened my laptop and pulled up my work from the morning. It seemed a lifetime ago that I'd written the words I was about to share. I transferred the document to a jump drive and returned to the main house.

Belle and Jake stood out front with their heads together. "You two look like you're scheming."

"Jake's given me a job. The Family Liaison Officer is held up in Land's End, and I'm to sit with Issa until she can get here. It's not the way I'd hoped to meet her, but I'm happy to help."

A look of relief appeared on Jake's face. "I can't think of anyone more suited to the task than Belle. The son wants to return to his room to place calls to the family lawyer and the victim's editor, and neither of us wants to leave Issa alone. With her nursing background, Belle's the perfect substitute, especially since the doctor hasn't arrived yet."

The table by the window in the library now had seven chairs around it for our critique group meeting. Claire welcomed Wendy as my co-author and reminded us of the flow and the ground rules. We would provide the context for our work and read aloud what we'd written that morning. The others would jot notes, share their feedback, and give their written comments to the writer. Claire would give the final response each time.

"Remember, we want honest but encouraging comments. Talk about what confused you or what passages held your attention. If it enters your mind to tell the writer how they should fix the problem, imagine me striking through your thought with a big red X."

I was thankful that Claire was playing hall monitor. It wouldn't take long to demoralize me if the words 'you should' cropped up over and over. Given that the group represented a variety of genres, I wondered how it would go. How, for example, would a thriller writer respond to a romance or a cozy mystery?

Volunteering to go first, Evie shared the setup for her novel, and where this piece fell in the flow. "This is a clean romance set in Brighton, and the main characters are middle-aged." A smile spread across my face as she read, and my notes covered how well I thought she captured the emotions of middle-aged love.

Dirk sat next to Evie and spoke first. "You won't be shocked to hear I neither read nor write romance, so I won't comment on those aspects. What struck me was the way you captured the seaside. I've been to Brighton, and I felt like I was there, as you described it."

His comments gave me hope that he wouldn't trash our cozy. Next up was Oliver, who labeled his book a gay romance featuring two male tennis players. I was an abysmal failure at tennis, but that didn't stop me from appreciating Oliver's vivid description of a fiercely competitive match.

Biting the bullet, I went next and explained that a cozy mystery meant no cursing, no sex on the page, and no blood and gore. "This morning, I shifted gears and rewrote the opening in first person, a change that means the amateur sleuths will take center stage instead of the constable."

Oliver commented that most cozies had a strong female lead, and that he thought my opening laid that foundation. Once again, Dirk focused on the setting and complimented me on evoking the feel of the Cotswolds with the description of the cottage's golden stone. "Is the black cat I saw wandering around last night the inspiration for Agatha?"

Wendy's response that we changed her name to protect her identity got a chuckle. Before I knew it, Claire wrapped up my feedback, and I felt my shoulders relax. I had come through my first critique meeting unscathed.

That left only Dirk and Nora, and Dirk volunteered. He'd set his latest thriller in Istanbul, and he was experimenting with opening with the chase scene. His protagonist was running through a crowded street market, and I was right there with him. I could picture the colorful displays of cloth, jewelry, and pottery as he ran for his life. I could feel the stifling heat.

The others echoed my reaction. Claire asked whether the plot would be linear or whether Dirk envisioned a flashback. It was all food for thought, as I considered my and Wendy's book.

Nora took us through the setup for her historical romance set in England between the world wars. Perhaps I was starstruck sitting among published authors, but I was hard-pressed to see ways to improve what she read. I looked forward to hearing Wendy's take later.

"Are we skipping Wendy?" asked Dirk, when Claire provided folders for us to tuck our critique pages into. She explained that Wendy and I were cowriters, and she might get a turn next time. I followed Wendy down the hall to her room, and we each flopped onto a bed. I'd half expected Jake to pull a writer out of the critique group to question and wondered why he hadn't.

Wendy stretched her arms above her head. "I bet he started with the journalist or Brax, since they aren't participants. No need to make one of the writers miss the critique session."

"True. So, be honest with me. What do you think of the opening for our cozy? Does it work for Lily to be the main character? What would you change?"

"Leta, I can't believe how insecure you are about your writing. It's as good as anything I could have written, and I loved the description of Christie, I mean Agatha, licking your face. My hesitation is Jonas. I know I'm the one who said to try writing it with you as the lead, but I'm rethinking that. He's so excited about being the star of the Constable James series, how can we disappoint him? I've been thinking, and I have a proposal."

When Wendy used the word proposal, I went on high alert. "Don't tell me it's Jake's case. We agreed we were taking a break from sleuthing, didn't we?"

"Excuse me. Who said it had anything to do with investigating? I'm fully on board with spending the week working on our book. I'm talking about our co-writing process. Will you shoot me if I ask you to try writing in Jonas's voice again? I can edit what you write each evening while you make notes for the next bit. The following day, you review my edits, adjust as you see fit, and write more. As we get into it, we may decide on a different approach, but let's give this a try."

Groaning about starting over again, I agreed she had a point. "That works, but why don't you also add ideas for the next day's section? That will help spur my thinking. Or we could alternate writing chapters." I left her jotting notes, and I went in search of Dave.

Brax stood at the intersection of the two hallways, looking toward the back patio. "Leta, have you seen your DI? I hope he's not still with my mother."

I tried to hide my frown. "Brax, he's not my DI. He's a friend, and I'm thankful it's him we're dealing with. I like his manner, and I respect his expertise. I've encountered way too many abrasive police officers."

"You make it sound as though you routinely deal with the law, Leta. What is it? Speeding tickets? Disturbing the peace?"

"Not hardly. I'm a very law-abiding citizen, but I've been close to several police investigations, not because I broke the law. I was just in the wrong place at the wrong time."

A perplexed look appeared on his face. "Humor me, Leta. What does that mean?" After a brief pause, his mouth dropped open. "Wait, I recall hearing last night that your plot comes from a real-life experience. Does that mean you've been involved in solving a murder?"

Not a connection I want bandied about. "My plot is about a dognapping ring, and I was involved because Dickens went missing."

"Okay, I can buy that, but you said 'several police investigations.' There must be more to the story."

The last thing I wanted was to get into a discussion about the murder investigations I'd been involved in. But if chatting with me distracted him from his father's death, I didn't want to brush him off. I did my best to portray the Little Old Ladies' Detective

Agency as a humorous hobby that occasionally veered too close to official investigations.

Hearing that we'd dubbed Dave the clueless old codger made him chuckle, but I could tell he was still curious. "Why am I struggling to see Dave as clueless and you as an innocent little old lady?"

"I'd like to think it's because you don't see me as old. Now, I'm off to find my old codger. Would it help if I checked on your mother while I'm going that way?"

He brushed his hand across his mouth. "Yes, please. I'm waiting for our lawyer to get back to me, and Dad's PR gal to send me a draft press release. We may need to engage a local solicitor to help us understand how to deal with an inquest and what all that entails. In a way, working on this is a welcome distraction. I may not have been close to Dad, but I wasn't prepared to lose him like this. He was old but healthy, except for the drinking. At least when my sister died, I was too young to understand."

He'd dropped two interesting details. He wasn't close to Trevor, and he had a sister who died. I wondered what part those facts played in the family dynamics I'd witnessed. He gave me his cell number, and I promised to let him know how Issa was doing.

Outside Willow Cottage, Jake and Belle were deep in discussion. The look on Belle's face told me she was arguing a point even before her words reached me. "No, Jake. She wants me to stay, and that's what I intend to do. Tell the Family Liaison Officer she can turn around and go home."

I couldn't hear Jake's low replies, but it was obvious he was losing the argument. "Do you two need a referee?"

Jake pulled out his phone. "No, Miss Marple here has already won. I know she's genuinely concerned about Issa, but I can also tell she's playing detective."

One hand on her cane and the other on her hip, Belle put him in his place. "Admit it, Jake, I've already discovered things you were unaware of. Wouldn't you agree that the more you know, the better off you are?"

My DI, as Brax had referred to him, ushered us toward my cottage. "Not here, Belle. Let's talk inside."

Surprised to find the cottage empty, I directed them to the seating area by the fireplace. "Belle, is Dickens still with Issa?"

"Yes, she finds us both a comfort. I provide tea and sympathy, and Dickens is like having a teddy bear at your feet. I got her to lie down for a rest, and she dozed right off. That's what she needs."

"There you go, Jake. Belle's the best caretaker anyone could ask for. Many's the time she's taken care of me and others. What concerns you about her talking to Issa?"

"Look, I trust you two, so I'll be honest. And I already know you'll tell Dave and Wendy, but that's as far as it needs to go for now. It doesn't look like an accident to me."

I pictured the broken fence railing. "I wondered whether he was so drunk that he staggered against the fence and fell—because of the empty whiskey bottle in his cottage. But I guess there's no reason to think he drank it all last night."

"I haven't asked the wife and son yet, but you're right. If he was drinking heavily, yes, he could have stumbled into the fence, causing it to give way, or he could have jumped. What I don't know is whether he was alone. Either way, I'm not ready to commit yet."

That made three possibilities. "And you're concerned that if it wasn't suicide or an accident, Belle might come across information that would endanger her? Is that it?" As I made that comment, I heard the back door open. It seemed my missing fiancé had returned.

"Yes, Leta. I don't for a minute think that Issa Wright attacked her husband. Her physical condition makes that unlikely. But if she knows anything that could point the finger at someone who might have, she could be in danger. And I'd rather Belle not be in the line of fire."

Ticking off names in my head, I counted fourteen people on the premises the previous night, including the victim. "So, if you eliminate Issa and Trevor, you have twelve suspects—five women and seven men."

I had a horrible thought about the likeliest suspect always being a family member. "You don't think it was Brax, do you?"

"He's high on my list. Something's off about his reaction to his father's death, and he has no alibi for last night. But it's early days yet. I've got George, the owner, three men who sat up half the night drinking plus Brax and Oliver, who, on the face of it, were in their separate rooms. And then there's Chef Duncan, who supposedly went home to Padstow last night."

"Seven men all together . . . but you know Dave didn't do it, so really it's six."

Jake had the grace to hesitate. "I've interviewed him, Leta, but you know I can't rule him out. The victim insulted both of you, and Dave admits he was furious with the man. It's clear from what's he's said that he doesn't remember much of last night. And he found the body."

As a blush spread across Jake's face, I felt two hands on my shoulders and heard a soft chuckle. "Is this where I get my new name tag—one that says, Dave Prentiss, Murder Suspect?"

CHAPTER NINE

AWKWARD DIDN'T BEGIN TO describe the situation. Jake tried to explain himself. Dave persisted in cracking jokes about the killer revisiting the scene of the crime, and Belle and I were caught in the middle.

"Enough," I said. "Dave may not have an alibi, but neither do I, Jake. You'll interview us and ascertain we don't have motives, and that will be the end of it. Unless, of course, you think a man insulting Dickens is a motive for me."

Thank goodness for Belle. "This is getting ridiculous. Jake, I think it's time we gave Dave and Leta time to themselves. Surely, you have more promising suspects to speak with for now."

I was fit to be tied when I closed the door and turned to Dave. "How can you joke at a time like this? Jake may be a friend, but if he sees you as a viable suspect, you could wind up in jail. Is it true you don't remember what happened last night?"

When he hesitated, I feared the worst. I struggled to calm my breathing, but visions of Torquay kept getting in the way. I had vivid memories of the Torquay police accusing me of murder, taking me to the police station, and interviewing me.

"Not exactly, Leta. I don't remember every bit of the conver-

sation. I can't say who came and went at what time, but I know
I was there until I climbed into bed here with you. I have fuzzy
memories, not memory gaps. So, there's only a small kernel of
truth in what Jake said."

He pulled me into a hug. "Dare I say that you're overreact-
ing?"

"That's as bad as telling me to calm down!"

"Whoa boy. I can tell that was a mistake. Why don't we sit
down with a glass of wine and talk through what I recall from
last night? After that, you can tell me if you still think I'm in
danger of being handcuffed and hauled off."

Finally, he'd said something that made sense. "That would
help."

He handed me a glass of wine. "Spike and I drifted back and
forth between trashing Trevor Tarkington and discussing our
writing careers. I learned we have a lot in common, given we
both did stints as crime reporters and now write in-depth articles
on authors and books. I planned to research more of his work
online today, but obviously I never got to that. The hottest topic,
though, was how despicable Snarkington can be."

"Snarkington! Is that what you call him?"

"Yes, but we didn't make it up. On his podcast, 'Tarkington
Talks Books,' he has a segment called, 'Snark Time.' After he
got a reputation for being mean-spirited and someone called him
snarky, he went with it."

"Let me guess. Social media picked it up, and more people
tuned in, right?"

"Yup. Instead of political snark, he delivers book snark. People
love it. Don't get me wrong. He also writes evenhanded reviews,
but it's the harsh ones that have made him."

I thought of all the authors who probably wanted to push him
off a cliff, but never had the opportunity. "It's a sad statement

about our society, isn't it? On radio and TV talk shows, it's the argumentative hosts who thrive. I guess it was inevitable that the style would find its way to the world of books."

"I count myself fortunate that my nonfiction book wasn't important enough for him to bother with. Spike told me, though, that Tarkington brought it up over cocktails. He told Spike that he read enough of *Barrie & Friends* to know it was one of those namby-pamby quasi-biographies. You heard him use that insult last night. It's one of his favorite digs."

"What else did you two talk about all that time? Come to think of it, what time did you come to bed?"

Dave rubbed his eyes. "That's one of those fuzzy memories. It may have been twelve or even one. I remember saying at some point that I needed to turn in, but who knows when that was?"

Hopefully, Spike's or Dirk's memory was better than Dave's. "Did you guys discuss books?"

"Oh yes. We had a great time comparing my passion for Golden Age authors to his love of Hemingway, Steinbeck, and Faulkner. Odd choices for a Brit, I thought. He said an American uncle turned him on to those authors."

Christie chose that moment to jump into Dave's lap. "Perfect timing, Christie. Do you think Jake would take your word for what time I climbed into bed?"

"That reminds me, Dave. Dirk Blackthorne mentioned you told him about Dickens and Christie. When did he show up?"

"Now, that's an interesting story. We bumped into him as we were leaving the library to shift to the big room up front. He was returning his room service dishes to the kitchen. Turns out he arrived in time for last night's goings-on but chose not to take part."

Why do I think he arrived later? Did he say that or did I assume it? "Why? Was he tired or feeling under the weather?"

"Nope. He told us he didn't want to risk being stuck in a conversation with Tarkington. He'd been a victim of the man's snark early in his career, and it was on a book that was near and dear to his heart."

"How so?"

"It was a fictionalized account of his grandmother's work with the French Resistance. He changed the names, but it was a true story. Tarkington labeled it more fantasy than anything else, and it broke his grandmother's heart to read the insulting review. Blackthorne had planned to develop other aspects of her story into another book with a different female lead but abandoned that idea. Even though he's been successful with his shift to thrillers, he's never forgiven Tarkington. I need to look it up. I like his writing, and it's hard to imagine his WWII book was bad."

"That reminds me of *Liberation*, the book about Nancy Wake, the French Resistance fighter. She was known as the White Mouse and was on the Nazi's most wanted list. In that case, though, the author kept her real name. Books about what people experienced in WWII never seem to fall out of favor."

Dave lurched forward in his chair, triggering an indignant screech from Christie. "Oh my gosh, Leta. I completely forgot about Dirk running into Tarkington. It's a good thing we're replaying last night."

Closing his eyes, he sat back. "It was when Dirk went to his room to get a bottle of whiskey. By that time, we'd finished off the bottle Claire gave us." He motioned toward me. "Don't give me that look. I know I drank too much."

"Ya think?"

"Never mind that. Dirk came back muttering that his luck had run out. Tarkington slammed out of a room as Dirk went down the hall. Of course, the man couldn't pass up an opportunity to make a snide remark. Something to the effect that Dirk wasn't man enough to sit in on the panel.'"

"Dave, you've just identified a potential murder suspect. Dirk's initial experience with Tarkington may not be recent, but when you add the latest encounter, it's the best motive for murder I've heard so far. To someone who doesn't know you, it might seem that you have a fresher motive, if you will—and that's the fact he insulted both of us during the panel discussion. But that would only be a motive for punching him in the nose, not killing him. Jake should know that's about as much your style as pistols at dawn."

Questions were popping up in my brain. Whose room had Trevor Tarkington emerged from? That person could be another suspect. What about Oliver, who Trevor had insulted at dinner? Did the others have history with him, too?

Dave's next comment told me I'd been quiet longer than I realized. "I can see the wheels turning in your head, Leta. You know you can leave this to me, right? You and Wendy are here to work on your book, not to solve a murder case."

"Funny, we had that conversation today. If you can believe it, even Wendy is reluctant to get involved. We're both committed to focusing on writing. But I need to hear that Jake's turned up a promising suspect before I can feel comfortable that you're in the clear."

When Dave sat mute, staring into the fireplace, I knew he was deep in thought. "Leta, what if I enlist Belle as my partner? She's getting close to Issa and is perfectly positioned to learn more about Brax and his father. She's good at probing. We can feed Jake information about the family dynamics, not to mention who else might have wanted Trevor out of the way."

I was torn. More and more, I was hesitant to involve myself in another investigation. But steering away from sleuthing when my fiancé was a suspect seemed just plain wrong. "Are you saying that a clueless old codger and a single, solitary little old lady can clear your name and solve the case? I can see that working, but I'd feel a lot better if I were a sounding board."

"That would work. You and Wendy take a back seat and let Belle and me be the lead investigators. In the evenings, after you've completed your writing assignments, we can bring you two up to speed. How does that sound?"

"You make the Little Old Ladies' Detective Agency sound like a bona fide business. And you're suggesting that the founding member should give you and Belle a chance to spread your wings. I say, let's do it."

I went to find Wendy and left Dave taking a shower. The main house was quiet as compared to the previous night. Evie and Nora sat in front of the fireplace, and Charlie was behind the desk, but that was it. Discovering that Wendy wasn't in her room, I was headed to the patio when Jake stepped out of the library.

"Just the person I need. It's time for you to tell me what you witnessed at the cliff." He ushered me into the library and closed the door. "Take it from the moment Dave called to you."

I was still irritated with him, but my responsible nature took over. Running through finding Brax and Dirk by the fireplace and getting to the cliff as fast as we could was easy. "Let me think about what I saw after Dave pointed down the beach."

Jake waited. He knew from experience that I absorbed details others didn't notice. I did it unconsciously, and it wasn't until I rewound a scene in my head that I saw it all.

"The look on Brax's face told me something was horribly wrong, even before he said it was his father down below. He was so pale. Thank goodness, there was a bench there."

Closing my eyes, I remembered the sky and the ocean. "Near

the edge, in the bracken, I thought I saw something glass in the sunlight. And the fence, with two horizontal pieces of wood—one was broken. Was it rotten? Did it break when Trevor leaned on it?"

"It's not rotten, Leta. What did you notice about the path?"

I squinted as I recalled the fence, the blue of the ocean in the distance, but not the path. "Nothing, Jake. What did I miss?"

"It appears there was a scuffle on the path. The gravel and dirt were disturbed—not dug up as if by an animal, more like kicked up. That tells me there was more than one person out there. Add the whiskey bottle—that's the glint you saw—and I think there was a fight, and the victim was pushed over, or at least shoved into the fence."

"Couldn't he have been drinking alone?"

"Yes. But the fence isn't rotten. It didn't break because he drunkenly leaned on it. It took force for it to break and for him to tumble through. Force from another person."

"Suspicious death," I murmured. "I'd almost rather you sent us all home."

He gave me a bemused look. "I know you. You'll get over that feeling. Have you forgotten you've already rattled off a list of suspects?"

"You're right. I can't help myself, but I don't want to get involved, Jake." Dave and Belle could do that.

"I don't want you to get involved either, but I could use your eyes and ears. Just tell me what you see and hear over the next day or two. Don't investigate, just be your usual observant self."

That was simple enough. Belle and Dave would take the lead, and Wendy and I could stay on the sidelines. "Okay. I can do that. Are you staying?"

"As soon as I interview the chef, I'm going to the station in Bude to see what the team has for me. I'll be back tomorrow."

On the back patio, Wendy and Oliver had pulled chairs up to the firepit, and Dirk and Spike stood off to the side.

Oliver caught my eye and waved. "Leta, I'm having a fascinating chat with your cowriter. We're debating the best point of view for your cozy mystery."

Pulling up a chair, I let them fill me in. Wendy was struggling with our latest shift back to Constable James as the lead. "I don't know, Leta. Maybe we could make Lily the lead in the Little Old Ladies' Detective Agency series."

"Wendy, we haven't written a single book yet, and you're talking about a second series. Are you nuts?"

She leaned toward Oliver. "I told you she'd say that. She's not sure we can do this."

"I didn't say that! I'm just concerned about biting off more than we can chew."

"Now, Leta," Oliver said, "hear us out. Since *The Canine Caper* is a true story about Dickens, I suggest you save it for the Little Old Ladies' series. Wendy tells me you have five or six storylines you could use with Constable James as the main character. I'm in favor of starting that series with *An Incident at the Inn*, with the dead magician. Cozy mystery readers would love that."

By now, I was sure Wendy knew what my reaction to that bombshell would be. Not only had she revealed that we were real-life amateur detectives, she wanted us to write an entirely different book. I wasn't sure which was more worrisome. *Just how many of our cases has she shared with Oliver?*

Still, a part of me knew she was right. "Wendy, you agreed that my first attempt with Constable James in the lead didn't flow. Why don't you try your hand at that, instead? I'll keep on with *The Canine Caper*, since it's about Dickens, and at the end of the week, we'll see if we like one series better than the other."

Dickens skidded to a stop at my side as we were debating first or third person, and I looked up to see Belle and Dave making their way toward us. "You know what, Dickens? Tonight, you get to join us for dinner. Charlie told me there was no reason to banish you to the front room. How does that sound?"

In the dining room, Brax sat by the window, phone in hand. Whispering to Dave that we should split up for dinner, I invited myself to sit with Dirk. Dave grabbed a seat with Brax, and Oliver followed him. When Belle asked Spike if she could join him and Claire, I surmised Dave had filled her in about the sleuthing arrangement. Wendy made a third at Nora and Evie's table.

Dinner was a quiet affair. Unlike the first night, there were no disruptions. After Chef Duncan made his appearance, and dessert was served, Claire shared the updated agenda.

"After hearing several suggestions about the schedule, I've changed up the agenda for the next few days. It will include all the same activities, but in a different order. We'll devote to-morrow to a day of sightseeing and save the evening for writing. That means we're pushing Dialogue Dynamics to Tuesday. The minibus for our trip to Perranporth and Zennor will depart at nine."

The group exhaled an enormous sigh of relief, and Oliver congratulated Claire on a brilliant idea. A day seeing the scenery featured in Poldark followed by the town where D. H. Lawrence had lived from 1915 to 1917 would take our minds off today's tragedy.

"Thank you, Oliver, but the credit goes to all of you. I appreci-ate your feeling free to speak up and offer ideas. Now, we agreed we would take tonight off, but I'm available if anyone would care for a one-on-one."

Wendy piped up. "Claire, may Leta and I see you first? We've got to iron out point of view and whose story we're writing, or we won't get anywhere this week." When Claire suggested we meet in the library, I breathed a sigh of relief. Having an honest-to-goodness editor weigh in would be a huge help.

After hearing us out, she provided her input. "Leta, your opening scene works well. Why don't you continue with Lily as the lead in *The Canine Caper* but have a different detective inspector for her to work with. Wendy, you tackle the opening scene for the other plot with Jonas James as the lead but use third person limited. Set them in two different locales—so there's no connection between the two books. You'll either revert to one series or have two to run with." It was comforting to know she concurred with the basic concept of our approach.

Wendy and I adjourned to her room, where she agreed to start with Constable James greeting someone like my alter ego, as she pulls up to the scene of the crime at the inn. We'd both been involved in solving the murder of Max the Magician, so she knew the storyline. I'd continue to refine Lily's voice. After an hour on our laptops, we read our work aloud. "Wendy, I like the way you describe Jonas's reactions, especially that he's rolling his eyes at the village busybody. Let's see where we land this week. I can see one series being a spinoff of the other."

It suddenly hit me that the topic of Trevor's murder hadn't come up at all. And I hadn't told Wendy about Jake considering Dave a suspect. I needed to put her in the picture.

When I reached the part about Dave and Belle working to identify the killer, Wendy knitted her brows. "Why am I hesitant? There's nothing that says the two of them aren't as capable as we are, but this would be a first." I let her ponder the idea for a moment. Whether or not she realized it, I was employing my favorite tactic—the pregnant pause.

It worked. "Okay. We can always jump in if they don't make any headway. I say let's give it twenty-four hours and see what they come up with. Shall we drink to that?"

I rolled my eyes at her suggestion of a nightcap. "Are you kidding? I can hardly keep my eyes open now. I'm crawling into bed with *Evans Above* to see if Rhys Bowen's writing inspires me. I doubt I'll last more than a page or two."

"Would you believe I brought *Constable on the Hill* to read? We'll have to compare notes tomorrow."

When I opened the door to my cottage, not a creature was stirring. Dave sat on the couch with his feet propped on the ottoman and his chin on his chest. Dickens lay at his feet, and Christie was curled in his lap.

I changed into my gown and robe and added a log to the fire before joining him. It wasn't until I laid my head on his shoulder that he stirred. "Hello, sweetheart. Did you get much writing done?"

"Enough. At least we made a start. I'm glad to see Dickens here. Did Brax return him?"

"Sort of. When I offered to take him for a walk, he suggested I let him sleep with us tonight." He held up a notepad. "I've been reading up on our fellow guests, including Issa and Trevor. It's amazing what you can find on the internet. What's difficult is figuring out what's true."

"Would you be disappointed if I wanted to wait until tomorrow to talk about it?"

"Heck no. Sleeping on it is a magnificent plan. Let's get up early enough to discuss it over coffee here before we go to breakfast. We can sort the wheat from the chaff and put together short bios on everyone—bios that help to explain the dynamics. Not the professional bios of who does what, but—"

"Who's connected to whom and how. I get it. I see an image of Trevor Tarkington in a circle in the middle of a page, with lines drawn to the others all around it. Just like Maisie Dobbs does."

"Right. Who knows? We could solve the case with one cup of coffee!"

I didn't want to burst his bubble, so I kissed him on the cheek and refrained from rolling my eyes.

CHAPTER TEN

WHEN I ROLLED OVER at six thirty, Dickens stuck his nose in my face. "We went for a run in the dark." He was damp, not wet, so I assumed the morning mist was thick.

Dave emerged from the bathroom with a towel wrapped around his waist. "Time's a-wastin', sleepyhead. Can I bring you a cup of coffee?"

"No thanks. I can tell you've got the fire going, so I'll meet you out there."

Joining me on the couch, he brandished his notepad. "I've gotten lots done this morning. I scanned my notes, thought about things while I ran, and laid it all out in a diagram before my shower."

Oddly enough, I was relieved not to be in charge. I could get used to this. "And what have you surmised, Tommy?"

"Well, Tuppence, let me tell you the back story on Issa and Trevor. It's kind of sad. As she mentioned that first night, they met at a literary conference. I didn't realize what a successful editor he was. He worked with lots of A-list authors.

"He was ten years older than Issa, and they married two years later, soon after she published her second children's chapter book. By the time their daughter Elizabeth was born, Issa was a household name—at least to parents of young children."

"Brax mentioned he had a sister who died. Was that Elizabeth?"

"That's the heartbreaking part. Elizabeth was diagnosed with leukemia and died when she was only five. Brax was two, I think."

"Oh, my goodness. That sends a chill down my spine. All I can see are those commercials for St. Jude's. Is that where they took her?"

"Yes. From what I could glean, Trevor had published one novel while still working as an editor. After the diagnosis, he turned to writing full time and gave up his editing job to stay home with Elizabeth. Of course, Issa was also at home writing, but she had a new baby to tend to, in addition to a sick toddler. I gather it was Trevor who made most of the trips to St. Jude's."

How do parents survive that? I'd given money to St. Jude's and the March of Dimes for years, but the closest I'd come to that kind of heartbreak was a distant cousin with cerebral palsy.

I took our mugs to the kitchen and refilled them. "Dave, did you make note of when Issa shifted from children's books to women's fiction?"

"No. Why?"

"I wonder whether she found herself unable to write happy adventure stories after Elizabeth died. Women's fiction would have allowed her to explore the joys and sorrows of adult life."

He jotted a note. "I'll check the timing later. You could be onto something. What I do know is that Trevor became prolific after Elizabeth's death. He churned out those detective novels of his like clockwork. Two of them became made-for-TV movies."

"And the podcast? When did that start?"

"About five years ago."

Coincidence or cause? "Wasn't Issa diagnosed with Parkinson's five years ago?"

"That sounds about right. And she hasn't put out a novel since. Why?"

"It's possible that Trevor's way of dealing with tragedy was to throw himself into work, first writing and then starting a podcast. Issa said something about him wanting to maintain the illusion that she was perfectly healthy."

He kissed me on the nose. "This is why two brains are better than one. I didn't think about the timing."

As we left the cottage with Dickens, we heard voices. Belle was pulling her hood over her head, while Brax held the umbrella for her.

Dickens trotted over and Dave called a greeting. "Would you and Issa like company this morning, Brax? We've had our run and now Dickens is ready to relax."

Brax's face lit up. "Mom would love that. Dickens can watch while I help her with her exercise routine, and then the two of them can sit in front of the fire while I work on finding a solicitor. We've got to get a handle on the repatriation process."

He must have noticed my questioning look. "I was in the dark too, Leta. I'd heard the word before but didn't know it meant getting a body back to the States. Between that and the inquest, we need expert legal advice."

Belle and I left the two men chatting and headed to the main house. "Did you sleep well, Belle? Or were you up checking on Issa all night?"

"No worries, luv. I slept fine. Issa takes meds to help her sleep, so despite the circumstances, she fell asleep quite easily. I passed the time rereading one of her books before I turned in. I suspect I'm looking for hidden meaning in it now that I've met her. Silly, I know."

"Oh, I don't know about that, Belle. They say authors should write what they know, so some of her life experiences are probably in there. It could be like Wendy and me writing a book with ourselves and our friends in it. Anyone who knows us will see who's who in a heartbeat."

She stopped me before I opened the door to the main house. "Leta, I want you to know how chuffed I am that you and Wendy are taking a back seat this time."

It took a moment for her comment to click. "Gosh, Belle. It's a weight off my shoulders. I know you two can find a way to eliminate Dave from the suspect list. If you do more than that, it will be a bonus."

Wendy and Oliver sat together at a window table, and we joined them. Oliver toasted me with his cup of tea. "Congratulations! I hear you sorted which point of view to use and which story to tell. I have a suggestion, though."

In mock horror, I clapped my hand to my chest. "Please, Oliver, not another change."

He motioned to Wendy. "Not for this week, dear. It's for later. After you've established these two series . . ."

"What does established mean? Three books in each one?"

"Possibly. There's no set rule. But, as I was saying, after you've done that, you could do a book with a crossover plot. Do you recall Robert B. Parker having Jesse Stone and Sunny Randall connect in one of his books?"

In a telltale sign she was considering the idea, Wendy scrunched her mouth to the side. "You know, we could do that. Brilliant, Oliver." All I could do was shake my head in dismay.

Dave appeared ten minutes later as Oliver was excusing himself. "Ladies, how goes it?" He looked at Belle. "I gather you're off duty this morning. Shall we put our heads together and compare notes while Wendy and Leta are off sightseeing?"

Belle beamed. "Yes. I've picked up several nuggets, and I'd like to hear what you learned by Googling Issa and Trevor."

After ordering a full English from George, Dave grabbed a piece of bacon from my plate. "I'm starving after my early morning run."

Belle shook her head of white curls. "Leta, why do I think he's starving most of the time?"

"Because he is. You can't believe how much I envy his metabolism. Not enough to take up running, mind you, but I *am* jealous."

"Mum," asked Wendy, "if you're off duty this morning, do you want to take the bus trip with us?"

"No, luv. I don't know that I can be spared all day. I'll be fine here, and Dave and I have important work to do."

Wendy choked on her tea. "Mum, you sound so official. Hopefully, whatever you two get up to, you'll find something that puts Dave in the clear."

Patting Wendy on the hand, Dave glanced at Belle. "I'm sure we will, Wendy, and if it turns out Belle has the afternoon off, we may drive to Boscastle and Padstow for our own tour. I found out that Padstow is on a list of the ten most picturesque villages in Cornwall."

When I pulled Wendy into the library, she raised her eyebrows. "Leta, are you thinking the same thing I am?"

"If it's that we have a ninety-minute bus ride that shouldn't go to waste, yes, I am. I know Dave and your mum are on the case, but there's no harm in us surreptitiously hearing what the others think."

"Agreed. We're not investigating. We're not taking time away from our writing. We're simply observing, like Jake asked you to. We can be opportunistic, but we should also try to cover our bases, right?"

"How so?"

"I've already spoken to Oliver more than once, so I'll focus on the romance writers. That only leaves Dirk. Can you handle him?"

"Me? Handle a dashing thriller writer? Sure." I might be engaged, but Dirk was a handsome man.

"It's a burden, I'm sure." She winked. "I bet you can surface details that Dave doesn't remember from that first night. As for Nora and Evie, I know a way to get them talking. I'll tell them the truth—or part of the truth. My book takes place at an inn, and I'd like to know what they think of the lodgings here."

"Awesome idea, Wendy. And you can describe the murder in the book and segue to what happened here. Are they horrified or intrigued or what? It's all background."

We were running to the minibus when Jake pulled up. "Whoa. Hold on, Leta. Is Dave already on the bus? And Spike?"

"No. Dave and Belle are in the dining room. They're working on pointing you in the right direction—as in away from Dave. And I have no idea where Spike is."

Jake pulled me aside. "Leta, you know I have no choice. The three amigos had so much to drink, their stories are all over the place. I'll sort it as soon as possible."

I had a flashback to the 1980s movie with Steve Martin, Chevy Chase, and Martin Short. If Jake could compare Dave, Spike, and Dirk to the three comedians, perhaps he didn't see them as serious suspects. "Are you looking at anyone else? Yesterday, Brax was high on your list."

That got me an eye roll. "Didn't I hear a rumor that you were going to write mysteries instead of trying to solve them?"

He turned toward Ash Cottage and motioned me on my way. "Enjoy your day and let me get on with my investigation."

Claire stood at the bus door, handing out bottles of water. As we boarded, she encouraged us to branch out, which fit perfectly with my and Wendy's plan. Evie and Nora had dutifully split up, and Evie invited Wendy to join her. With Nora already paired with Oliver, I snagged the seat next to Dirk.

Holding the mic, Claire introduced the day. "Good morning. Today, we'll explore an area of Cornwall where two authors lived—Winston Graham, the author of *Poldark*, and *War Horse* author Michael Morpurgo. D. H. Lawrence also lived there, but not for nearly as long as these two. Spike O'Malley was kind enough to provide copies of the articles he wrote on all three."

The folders she passed out held not only the articles but also maps and other tourist material. "Spike told me where to look for signaling spots used by smugglers, so we'll walk far enough on the St. Ives to St. Just path to take in a few of those. It seems our ace crime reporter did a bit of kayaking and caving in the area in his youth. There, we'll be able to see signaling spots allegedly used during times of smuggling. When we're thirty minutes out from Perranporth, I'll share more about Winston Graham's prolific writing career."

We hadn't gone far before Dirk asked how Dave was doing, a question that led nicely to my inquiries about the evening the three amigos had spent together. "How is it, Dirk, that you didn't seem as hungover as Dave? I hear it was you who fetched the second bottle of whiskey."

He winked. "Fetching whiskey doesn't equate to drinking it. I sipped, but I couldn't keep pace with Spike, and Dave should have given up long before he did. It was an entertaining evening. I'll say that."

"Dave tells me you purposely missed the panel discussion so

you wouldn't have to see Trevor Tarkington, but you bumped into him later."

The police didn't have the luxury of gathering clues this way, but people divulged much more in casual conversation than they did when an officer was firing questions at them. That was my and Wendy's secret weapon. It would be interesting to see if I would walk away with something useful that Jake didn't know.

"I try to schedule one conference or workshop every year, and I chose this one so I could get a feel for Harris House. But I never would have signed up for the bloody thing if I'd known he'd be here. He was a last minute add, but I thought if I avoided the first night, I'd be home safe."

"Was there bad blood between you two? After seeing him in action on the panel, I can only imagine."

"From what I hear, his act during the panel was nothing compared to what he's like on his podcast or in his written reviews. It's ancient history, but he skewered me over my second historical fiction book, and I couldn't see my reputation in that genre ever recovering. Thank goodness, he's never gone after my thrillers."

He told me much the same story Dave had, about his grandmother as a resistance fighter. "Sure, I invented dialogue for my gran and her fellow fighters, and I put words in the mouths of the Germans who tracked them. I changed all the names, except for those of the German commanders. It devastated my gran when he used the word fantasy to describe it. Every encounter was true, down to scrounging for food, and crawling through the woods—even the crescent-shaped scar on Gran's knee."

The anguish in his voice made it sound as though he'd lived it, not merely written it. "Have you ever considered returning to that genre? Your passion for it is obvious."

"It's odd. My first book was also a WWII story, just not as personal. It got fair to middling reviews and, fortunately, didn't attract Snarkington's attention. I used my real name for both."

He stared out the window for a moment. "When I read up on Claire, I wondered about resurrecting the books, perhaps with new covers. I know Harris House publishes both military history and historical fiction. But then I ran into Trevor Tarkington."

"And?"

"He knew right away who I was. He must have researched the workshop participants, because he knew two of my thrillers had briefly hit the USA Today bestseller list. 'At least your flair for fantasy works better there than in historical fiction,' he said. The gall of the man."

"Good grief, Dirk. How did you react?"

"I wanted to slug him, but instead I brushed past him without a word. Not that I wasn't muttering, but I wasn't going to give him the satisfaction of reacting. The man thrived on conflict."

"And you didn't let him drive you to drink too much—the way he did Dave."

"He got to Dave. But I hear he didn't let it show until after the panel discussion. And Tarkington will never have the satisfaction of knowing how much Dave drank that night." He stroked his goatee. "And you know what, now that he's out of the way, I may get serious about talking to Claire. Dave thinks highly of her as an editor."

There it was. A motive at least as plausible as Dave's. The man had trashed his writing, provoked him to leave behind a subject he was passionate about, and could have stood in the way a second time.

After encouraging him to speak with Claire, I asked another question about the whiskey-fueled night in front of the fire. "Do you recall who left first that night? Spike or Dave, or you? I still can't believe Dave went for a run the next morning."

"The good news for Dave is that he left us 'round about

midnight, soon after I'd shared my gran's story. We might have had to carry him out if he'd stayed any longer. You know, misery loves company, so Spike and I carried on."

In a short twenty minutes, I'd earned my keep by getting not only Dave's departure time but also details on Dirk's book. I hoped Wendy's chat with Evie was equally fruitful.

After an hour, Claire gave her talk about Winston Graham. I had no idea the author had moved to Perranporth at age seventeen and spent most of his adult life there. When I texted Wendy that I'd never read any of the Poldark books, she admitted she hadn't either.

"How odd is that?" she texted. "Did you watch the series in the '70s?"

"Yes, but not the reboot, and I never really thought about where it was filmed. Who would have thought I'd one day see the places in Perranporth that were on TV?"

The other thing I hadn't known was that Graham also wrote thrillers and that Hitchcock's *Marnie,* starring Tippi Hedren and Sean Connery, was based on his novel of the same title. When Claire asked what stood out for us about the movie, I blurted, "Sean Connery."

Evie elaborated on my answer. "And a young Sean Connery at that. Cor, the man was handsome."

"Come now," said Claire, "aren't there any votes for Tippi Hedren or the writing?"

Dirk offered his opinion. "Sorry, Tippi Hedren never did a thing for me, but there's no question that Graham's exploration of psychological themes was well done, and Hitchcock did an equally stellar job of it in the movie."

In Perranporth, we strolled the beach where the coastal scenes in *Poldark* were shot, and I had the overwhelming sense of being transported to a different time and place. Seeing the stretch of golden sand stretched between dramatic cliffs, I could close my eyes and imagine horses galloping across the beach as the waves pounded the shore.

The Wheal Coates Tea Room, where we ate lunch, afforded another breathtaking view of the rugged coastline. Wendy and I shared a table for four with Claire and Dirk, who dove deep into the topic of Winston Graham's first book, written in 1934. They described *The House with the Stained Glass Windows* as a mystery with elements of romance.

"You might enjoy it, Leta, since you're writing a gentler mystery," said Dirk. "Some critics labeled it predictable, but I think it's well done. Of course, I much prefer his thrillers."

Claire agreed. "It's all about taste. To me, it has elements of early Mary Stewart, except it's darker. Which makes me think, ladies. Will your mysteries have any romance in them?"

Looking at me, Wendy winked. "If we follow the mantra to write what we know, they'll have to. Since you suggested Leta try writing in first person with her alter ego as the lead, I see her adding a Dave-like character to the story."

The question of just how closely the character would resemble Dave triggered a laughter-filled discussion. Would he have thinning hair or the beginnings of a potbelly? Or would he be suave and debonair with a killer smile? We all agreed it would be too boring to merely describe him as he was.

Next up was the thirty-minute trip to Zennor. On the way, Claire told us about D. H. Lawrence living in the cottage now inhabited by Michael Morpurgo. He'd lived there with his German wife Frieda before being accused of signaling enemy submarines and being expelled from the county in 1917.

Using Spike's information, Claire pointed out three signaling spots on our short walk along the St. Ives to St. Just path. As we stood atop a cliff, she first pointed out to the ocean and then straight down, explaining that just below us was a sea cave used for smuggling. "I can't say that I've ever seen it, but Spike tells me he explored it on one of his kayaking adventures. Can't you just picture crates of rum stored inside back in the day, with a grizzled guard smoking a pipe?"

When my phone pinged with a text from Dave, I showed Wendy. "Looks like your mum will get to explore after all. They're on their way to Padstow and plan to visit the restaurant where Chef Duncan works and explore the town before heading to Boscastle."

"I bet they think they'll pick up a clue that points to Chef Duncan as a suspect. Like Trevor Tarkington gave a scathing review to the Coastal Kitchen, so our chef pushed him off the cliff."

"Is this where I say stranger things have happened? Still, you never know. Something they see or hear could trigger a random aha."

On the return trip to Port Isaac, I sat by Oliver, knowing I'd have to find out what I could before I dozed off. I opened with how well Wendy's first chapter for *The Incident at the Inn* was going and thanked him for suggesting we try it. "It's eerily reminiscent of what's happened at the Clifftop Retreat, except the dead man in our books is a magician, not an author."

Oliver grimaced. "Does he deserve killing as much as Trevor Tarkington? Or is he likeable?"

In a movie, my gasp would have been audible, but I disguised it with a cough. "He doesn't have any redeeming qualities at all. Do you think that's too predictable? I mean, does the victim always deserve to be done away with?"

"I see it as acceptable to kill off deserving or innocent characters if the motive works. For Trevor Tarkington, I imagine any number of people would have been happy to do him in. The issue is that they're not all here. That narrows the field, doesn't it?"

I agreed it did, and I shared the remark he'd made about Dickens and mongrels. "That might be a motive for me to throw a drink in his face, but not much more. What about you, Oliver? He said something insulting to you at dinner, but you didn't know him before that, did you?"

"No, thank goodness. And like you, I would have loved to throw that drink, but I'm not that kind of person. Nor am I someone to throw a punch. I admired Dave for keeping his cool that night. Tarkington's comments were out of line."

I put on my best distraught face. "I'm worried about that, Oliver. The police seem to think that interaction makes Dave a suspect. Plus, he found the body. What I wouldn't give for the finger to be pointed elsewhere."

Oliver patted my hand. "Leta, I don't want to point the finger at anyone at all, but I can't be the only one who heard Brax arguing with his father. If nothing else, that should be enough to muddy the water for the police."

"Do you mean the loud voices as they left the library that night? I picked up the tone, though I didn't catch the words."

"No. It was later in Brax's room. My room is adjacent to his, so I heard it loud and clear. How the man could berate his son for spending too much time playing nursemaid to his mother, as he put it, is beyond me. He should have been down on his knees thanking him for taking care of his wife. Tarkington acted as though she had set out to ruin his life. As though the woman came down with Parkinson's to spite him. What a miserable sod."

"Did he slam the door when he left, Oliver?" He nodded. "Well then, you're right, someone else also heard the argument. Hopefully, the police are taking all this into consideration."

As the coastal scenery flashed by, I tried to make sense of the data I'd gathered, but it wasn't long before I drifted off. Claire's voice woke me. She was giving us the promised background on Michael Morpurgo. "Who saw *War Horse*?" We all raised our hands. "How many of you know the book was a children's book?"

Stunned reactions echoed around the bus. She informed us that while the author had written adult books, he was best known for his children's books and had won both the Carnegie Medal and the Children's Laureate award for his works. Published in 1982, *War Horse* told the story of Joey, a horse drafted into service as a war horse in World War I.

Nora's words captured my feelings about the movie. "How do you describe the experience of seeing a movie that's well done and moving, but far too gut-wrenching? I can't say, 'I enjoyed it,' even though the ending was heartwarming with Joey surviving the war and coming home to England."

As we pulled into the parking lot of the Clifftop Retreat, Claire reminded us that cocktails would start at six, and that we'd have the evening off to write after dinner.

"Wendy, I see my car is back. Shall we see what kind of day your mum and Dave had?" Her answer was to stretch and follow me.

At Ash Cottage, the two were hard at work at the kitchen table. I kissed Dave on the cheek. "Are you in the clear yet?"

"No, but we're making decent progress." He held up Issa's book, *Summer Solstice*. "When I told Belle about the Tarkingtons losing their daughter, she remembered there was a subplot in this book about a child with cancer. She's looking for other similarities."

Belle pointed to her notes. "I've also found out what Brax does for his mum and dad. In explaining to me how indispensable Brax is, Issa's revealed a lot about the family dynamics. Not only does he handle their finances and their correspondence, he also functions as a research assistant, mostly for Trevor's detective novels—or he did."

I thought about how attentive he was to Issa. "So, was he as close to his father as he seems to Issa?"

Dave and Belle exchanged glances before she responded. "That's the confusing part. I think Issa wants to believe the two were close, but the brief exchanges I've had with Brax tell me something different.

"When he came by last night to check on his mum, she was already asleep, and we spent time together in front of the fire. As if it's not bad enough that his father died, he's learned that his father wasn't up-front with him about his latest book."

"How so?"

Dave summarized the situation. "Brax knew his dad was behind schedule, which wasn't all that unusual for him. What he didn't know was that he'd been putting his editor off for three months. Brax only found out when he contacted the man yesterday to tell him about his father's death. The first thing the editor asked, after offering condolences, was whether Brax had the updated manuscript with the new ending."

"But I thought he handled Trevor's correspondence. How could Brax not know?"

Belle frowned. "Trevor insisted on handling all correspondence with his editor. He even had a separate email account for that. Who knows why? Brax respected his father's privacy and never checked that account. Only after books were in production and events were being scheduled did he get involved. And, as he said, he handled everything else—the correspondence from fans and the hate mail from other authors."

Wendy had a puzzled look. "Hate mail? What am I missing?"

I'd forgotten that neither Belle nor Wendy had witnessed

the panel discussion, nor had they heard Dave's description of
Trevor's review style. Belle had an inkling after talking to Brax,
but Wendy was clueless. Dave gave them the short version of
Trevor's Snarkington routine.

Questions tumbled through my brain. "You've given us plenty
to digest. Should we plan an official meeting of the Little Old
Ladies' Detective Agency for tonight? After, of course, Wendy
and I get some writing done?"

Dave gave me a stern look. "Please remember who's in charge
of this case, Tuppence. You're right, though—a meeting is in
order."

CHAPTER ELEVEN

I THOUGHT THE LOLs would be the last ones to cocktails after our impromptu conference, but only Evie and Nora were in the front room when we arrived. They didn't look any perkier than I felt, and we all agreed it had been a long day.

Things weren't any livelier in the dining room, and it was almost a relief when Claire sent us off to write with a reminder that we'd kick off Tuesday with Dialogue Dynamics.

With a yawn, I suggested to Wendy that we use her room again to write. "Let's commit to an hour and join Dave and your mum after that. By then, my brain will be pretty much useless, so I'll be counting on those two to carry the conversation."

The sitting room, with Dave and Belle enjoying the fire, was a cheerful sight. Yawning, I took in the blank sheets of paper adorning the walls. "I'm going to be hard-pressed to keep my eyes open."

Wendy looked aghast. "You've got to stay awake long enough

to hear what I learned from Evie. Did you know that she and Nora have a cottage too? It's named Sycamore, and it's on the other side of the Tarkingtons' cottage."

"Ash, Willow, and Sycamore," said Belle. "What a lovely way to identify the cottages."

"Yes, Mum, it is. As for what Evie had to say, she explained that she and Nora told most of this to Jake, but talking it through with me brought more detail to mind. Just like on the telly when the officer says, 'I know we've been over this before, but people recall additional details the second time around.' That's a technique we should mention in our books."

Evie and Nora had heard loud arguing at the Tarkington cottage and were sure it had been two men and a woman.

That made me think of Oliver hearing angry voices. "Wendy, Oliver told me Trevor argued with Brax in his room, so I wonder whether the quarreling at the cottage came before or after that."

"I bet it was after because Brax wouldn't have let Issa walk alone to her cottage. Trevor must have been awfully angry if he followed Brax back to the inn."

Dave wrote the word Relationships on the paper. "Could the ladies make out what was said, Wendy?"

"Only random bits, but they pieced it together. Who knows how accurate it is? Trevor was furious that Issa was writing a new book. He said Brax was worthless as anything other than a nursemaid and there was something about waning years, but they couldn't figure it out. Someone slammed out of the cottage. They thought it was Brax because the arguing continued, and that couldn't have been Brax and Issa. At least, that was their take."

I recalled my conversation with Oliver. "Trevor must have had a real bee in his bonnet about Brax taking care of Issa. Oliver heard the same word, nursemaid. And we all saw his shock about

Issa's new book, but why was he furious?"

Belle had an answer. "Jealousy and selfishness. He wrote popular detective novels but nothing of the caliber of Issa's women's fiction. Issa intimated to me that Trevor wanted her to give up writing altogether to focus on her health, and he must have thought she had. Only she and Brax knew about the new book because he types up her dictation. Can you imagine being a writer and no longer able to type? As for his issues with Brax, I have no idea."

Interesting. Issa had commented that Brax's support helped her husband maintain the illusion that she was still young and healthy. But his wanting her to stop writing was a sign that he was aware of the toll her Parkinson's was taking.

By now, Dave had written Issa / Trevor—jealousy and Parkinson's below the word Relationships. Beneath that, he wrote Brax and sister. Brandishing the magic marker, he turned to face us. "I have an idea about Brax and his father. It's about Elizabeth."

That got Wendy's attention. "Who's Elizabeth?" She folded her arms. "I hate being out of the loop."

Dave recapped his internet discoveries about Elizabeth, the older sister who died at age five, when Brax was only two. "I had lunch with Brax today and asked him about her. Naturally, he doesn't have many memories of Elizabeth. He was too young, but he seemed inclined to talk about his family, and I let him."

He winked at me. "You know, Leta, I learned from the master that a pregnant pause will prompt people to talk. After years of family therapy, it became apparent that Trevor's coldness to Brax stemmed from his grief over Elizabeth's death. At least, that's the simplistic conclusion—that he wouldn't let himself get attached to Brax for fear he'd lose him too."

This was territory that Belle always shied away from. "You know I detest messing about in psychology. Can we just say that father and son were never close and leave it at that?"

Wendy pursed her lips. "Mum, I know how you feel about the topic, but it helps to know the why of their relationship and how the lack of warmth manifested itself. If Trevor was simply detached, that's one thing. If he resented Brax or was hostile to him, that's another."

"There's more," Dave said. "Brax didn't always work for his parents. After seeing his success in his marketing career, Trevor floated the idea of Brax putting his skills to work for him and Issa. One thing led to another, and shortly after Issa's diagnosis, he went to work for them full-time. Father and son respected each other and had a decent working relationship."

That shocked me. I hadn't considered how Brax came to work for his parents. "He can't possibly be making what he earned at a marketing firm, can he?"

"We didn't get into that, Leta. What was most interesting to me was how their relationship deteriorated as Issa's Parkinson's worsened."

In a way, that didn't surprise me. "How did Brax explain it?"

"You're going to label it pop psychology again, Belle, but Brax thought he knew why. You know the saying 'déjà vu all over again'? Brax is sure the thought of losing Issa stirred up the grief from losing Elizabeth. Trevor alternately pushed Issa away or tightened his grip. In Brax's case, Trevor distanced himself to the extent they hardly saw each other and communicated primarily via email and text. This has been going on for several years, even though Brax has an office in the Tarkingtons' Boston brownstone."

Wendy furrowed her brow. "Did he distance himself so much that he walled off whole areas of his life from him? That would explain why Brax can't locate a more recent version of the latest book. In a bygone era, I could imagine Trevor squirreling away a typed manuscript, but not nowadays, when authors use computers. Could it mean that he hasn't touched it in months?"

Grasping his neck, Dave feigned horror. "A typewriter! Heaven forbid. Yes, Cormac McCarthy and Danielle Steele have always used typewriters. Who knows why? But it would be odd for someone like Trevor to abruptly shift to using one. I wonder if he even owned a typewriter."

I recited what we knew about the relationship and asked the key question. "We know Trevor was distant to Brax, possibly even abrasive. But is that a motive for murder?"

"Not in my mind, Tuppence, but I get the feeling Brax is still high on Jake's list, right up there with me. Jake was more interested in quizzing me than in sharing specifics about the investigation."

Dave must have seen something in my face. "I'm not worried about it, Leta. He'll figure out soon enough that it's not me. Meanwhile, what did you learn today that might point the finger elsewhere?"

"I spoke with Dirk and Oliver. Nothing I heard from Oliver gave me any reason to view him as a suspect, but I think we could stand to dig into Dirk's early writing career. After hearing how badly Tarkington's criticism wounded his grandmother, I can't believe he chose to come to this event. He claimed he came to get a feel for Harris House, but he could have done that with a visit to their London office. It wouldn't have been quite the same, but in his shoes, I'd have canceled to avoid running into my archnemesis." I rolled my eyes. "Archnemesis—that makes them sound like Superman and Lex Luthor."

Pointing at me, Wendy giggled. "And Leta can be Lois Lane, right? Okay, I'm clearly so tired I'm slaphappy. Tell us what you learned in Padstow today."

Belle beat Dave to the punch. "That's easy. First, they have a delightful toy shop, and we found just what we needed."

"What were you doing in a toy shop, Mum?"

"Looking for something that would work for capturing notes. There were no office supply stores with those large Post-it thingies you girls like, but we found a large sketchpad in the toy shop that will do the trick. And next we discovered an ice cream shop!"

"Excuse me, Miss Marple, I believe Wendy was asking about the case, not my sugar habit. I'm not sure this is worth noting, but we learned that Chef Duncan is a celebrity in Padstow for his culinary skills, and he's also an involved member of the community."

"Dave's right. Everywhere we dropped his name, people had good things to say about him. Hometown boy who returned to Padstow after culinary school and stints at well-known restaurants in London."

"And here Leta and I were sure you'd uncover a deep dark secret that would put him at the top of the suspect list, Mum." She stood and stretched. "How is it that you got the afternoon off, anyway?"

"Brax and Issa had an afternoon appointment with a solicitor in Bude, and they looked done in when they got back. Not only Issa, but Brax too. Can you imagine having to deal with the ordeal of getting your husband's remains back to another country? It must be a nightmare."

Thank goodness I didn't have to deal with that when Henry died. I stood and stifled a yawn. "Now, I can't stay awake another minute. Is there anything else to cover tonight?"

Belle leaned on her cane. "Not from my end. I'm not sure how much progress we've made, but I need to get next door to relieve Brax. Perhaps I'll find out more about what they heard today. And did I mention Issa promised me a surprise? I can't imagine what it could be."

We were a livelier group at breakfast than we'd been the night before and were all seated and ready at nine when Claire kicked off Dialogue Dynamics. This was unfamiliar territory for me, and I was glad Claire provided handouts. Once again, I scribbled notes as fast as I could. Dialogue tags, pacing and rhythm, and show, don't tell—those were terms I'd heard but hadn't entirely grasped.

The good news was that I was already doing some of these things well, even if I didn't know what to call them. With my new understanding, I could see areas for improvement, and I planned to review what I'd written and incorporate this morning's tips.

Wendy and I were energized. "Wow, Wendy. I've read up on how to write dialogue, but Claire's explanations and examples made sense of it for me."

"You're right. And it triggered an idea for me on how to tackle the next scene with Constable James and his irritating boss. I can't wait to get started."

Looking for privacy and a comfortable writing space, we crossed the hall to the dining room and grabbed separate tables. We agreed to write for an hour and then compare notes. Save for the tapping of our fingers on our keyboards, all was quiet.

Wendy looked up first. "Ready? May I start? I can't wait to hear what you think of this scene where Jonas's Detective Chief Inspector berates him. It may remind you of someone in real life." I knew right away that she had channeled the DCI she'd briefly dated.

"Since you knew a particular DCI quite well, I bet it will. Let's hear it."

We went back and forth reading aloud the morning's work and were quite pleased with ourselves. I pictured us sitting side by side for the rest of the week as our stories took shape. With any luck, we'd be well on our way to two books by the time we returned home. Things were looking up, at least on the writing front.

We had time to spare before we grabbed our box lunches and boarded the minibus. Our afternoon destination was Fowey, home to author Daphne du Maurier and the inspiration for several of her novels. Dinner back at the inn would be a buffet, to allow time that evening for another critique group meeting.

"Leta, we've got thirty minutes. Let's check on Mum and Dave to see where they are with their detective work this morning."

Only Dave and Christie were at Ash Cottage. Christie was stretched out on the kitchen table where Dave sat with his laptop and notebook. "Hello ladies. Are you ready to regale me with dialogue tips?" He scribbled something in his notebook and leaned his chair back on two legs. "Or, better yet, are you going to read me what you've written today?"

"That would spoil the fun, Tommy. We dropped by to see whether you had any news. Is Belle with Issa?"

"I have some news, not much, and Belle's on duty next door. Brax has gone to Bude again to meet with the solicitor."

Somehow, that didn't sound good. "Boy, this repatriation thing must be a bear if it takes two days of meetings."

"Unfortunately, it's more than that. Given the questions Jake's been asking Brax and the number of times he's met with him, Brax is meeting with a criminal solicitor too. You can't believe all the different aspects of law that are involved. Coronial law for the inquest, family law for the repatriation—and surely the scariest, criminal law to protect Brax's rights."

Folding one arm across her stomach, Wendy cupped her chin in her other hand. "What about Issa? How is she holding up with all this going on?" She turned to me. "Didn't you tell me that stress could exacerbate her Parkinson's?"

"Yes, which makes me glad your mum's with her. What will you do while we're in Fowey, Dave?"

"Right now, I'm researching Thomas Hardy and Boscastle after our trip there yesterday. Spike mentioned visiting Port Isaac for fishing gear, and I may go with him. You know me. I'll keep myself occupied."

I shooed Wendy off and said I'd catch up with her. "Dave, I can't help but be glad Jake is more focused on Brax than he is on you, but what do you think? You've spent time with Brax. Do you see him as the top suspect?"

"I don't want to, but he has the best motive—his relationship with his dad and the likelihood that he and Issa stand to inherit. There's still Dirk to consider with the Snarkington review. And we haven't found anything to rule Spike in or out. None of the four of us have alibis."

"And, unfortunately for you, Jake sees Tarkington's comments during the panel discussion as a motive for you. Not to mention your unfortunate response to Oliver about all bets being off if he insulted me again. Though in the scheme of things, what he did to Dirk seems a whole lot worse. If only you had an alibi."

He rocked his chair to the floor. "Leta, at least Dirk gave you an approximation of when I left. We'll find something else. Don't worry. Now, off you go. Enjoy the afternoon."

My brain told me there wasn't much I could do to establish an alibi for Dave, but my heart urged me to stay behind. Would an afternoon with a master of suspense trigger a brainstorm?

CHAPTER TWELVE

WENDY AND I AGREED we would live in the moment, at least for the length of the tour. Discussion of suspects, solicitors, or alibis would be strictly off limits. With no sleuthing agenda in mind, I allowed myself to doze off on the ninety-minute drive.

Our first stop was the Daphne du Maurier Literary Centre followed by a guided walking tour of the town. Next was a scenic walk that provided a view of Menabilly, the estate that inspired Manderley in *Rebecca*.

"Leta," said Oliver, as he caught up with me on the path, "I picked this up for Dave. It's a brochure for the Daphne du Maurier Festival of Arts and Literature that takes place each May. He may want to inquire about attending as a speaker. I've been twice, and I can see him giving a talk about *Barrie and Friends*."

"Aren't you the most thoughtful man? Thank you." Fowey was a town Dave and I wanted to know more about. "As often as you've visited, you don't, by chance, know of any wedding venues around here, do you? I picked up a handful of brochures, but nothing leaped out at me."

"Nothing comes to mind, but I'll think about it." He winked at me. "Surely there's a castle somewhere around here that would do."

Our last stop was for a tour of Restormel Castle, whose ruins allegedly inspired *The House on the Strand*. We all congratulated Claire on outdoing herself in organizing the afternoon.

The clouds had been lazily rolling in for a few hours, and it began to sprinkle as we approached the Clifftop Retreat. With little time to spare before cocktails, I dashed to my cottage to change into a warmer top.

Only Christie greeted me. "It's about time you got here. Dave's been out all afternoon, and Dickens is next door again. Doesn't anyone care about me?"

"Of course we do, princess. Are you hungry?" If she could have put her tiny paws on her hips, she would have.

Once I'd given her a dab of wet food, I changed clothes and added lipstick. It was amazing how red lips could perk up a tired face. "Christie, do you want more food, or do you want to come with me?"

She was at the door in a flash, so she couldn't have been that hungry. At the main house, Hagrid meowed a greeting, and the two darted off. The roaring fire was a welcome sight, and cocktails were in full swing in the front room. When Dave spied me from across the room, he poured a second glass of red wine.

My first sip gave me a false sense of energy, but I knew it would pass. Too many late nights were taking their toll. The good news was that I wasn't dreading the critique group meeting as I had the first time. My confidence about my writing was growing. The bad news was it meant another late night.

Dave caught me stifling a yawn. "Now, Tuppence, you're not going to bail on our meeting tonight, are you?"

"No. I'm dying to hear what happened here today, and Wendy and I have things to share, too. Is Belle still with Issa?"

"Only through the cocktail hour. Brax had Issa's meal delivered early, and he and Belle are both joining us tonight for dinner. Dickens has been a big hit over there, and he'll keep her company until Brax returns. Guess what I did this afternoon, while Belle was next door?"

I whispered in his ear. "I thought you were researching Thomas Hardy. Did you also do some detective work?"

"No. I went into Port Isaac with Spike. He brought the rods he uses for river fishing but needed heavier fishing line for what he's likely to hook from the beach. The Port Isaac hardware store is like one of those old-time hardware stores I grew up with—filled with all kinds of odds and ends."

Spike appeared from out of nowhere and clapped Dave on the back. "Did he mention we also shopped for a laser pointer? You should've seen the look on the clerk's face. She said she'd seen videos of cats chasing laser dots, but they didn't carry the pointers."

When Belle walked up during this exchange, Dave looked relieved. "Tell her, Belle. You were insistent that I get a pointer for Christie. Even though I searched every shop in Port Isaac, I came up empty-handed. I was so disappointed, I had to hit the ice cream shop."

"Oh, you poor thing," she said. "And how many scoops did you have?"

"Not as many as Spike."

"Way to throw me under the bus, Dave. Can I help it if I have a healthy metabolism?"

I glanced from one to the other. "First, it's a night of drinking. Then, it's a day of ice cream binging. I'm afraid to ask what's next."

Dave winked at Spike. "An activity that doesn't involve eating or drinking, unless we're successful."

At my puzzled look, Spike elaborated. "Given the circumstances, I won't get as much time with Issa as planned. Since I've got some free time, I plan to get in a spot of fishing, and I've invited Dave to join me if he can. Who knows? We could ask the chef to cook mackerel or flounder for dinner."

Brax joined us in time to hear the fish comment. "Fresh seafood for dinner? That would be a treat. How was Fowey, Leta?"

"All I could have asked for. It's easy to see why images from Cornwall figure in so many of du Maurier's books."

I invited Brax to sit with Dave and me so I could tell him about the du Maurier tour. He said his mother had been looking forward to that excursion, and he might take her before they left for the States. "I know it sounds odd given my father just died, but I don't see us getting back to England after this trip."

What seemed odd to me was that he was in good spirits. I didn't want to ask, but I hoped that meant he felt good about his meeting with the solicitor.

He leaned in. "Mother's holding up well, so much so that she's asked me to escort her to the critique group meeting tonight." He winked. "Her and Dickens, that is." That was a surprise.

As I ducked down the hall to the powder room, I glimpsed Issa and Dickens at the front desk. I took it as a good sign that she had both the stamina and confidence to make the walk on her own. Dickens ran my way as Issa handed Charlie a thick stack of paper, and I lifted his ear and whispered, "She needs you. I'll see you in a little while."

By the time I returned, Brax was by his mother's side admonishing her. "I was on my way. You could have waited."

"Brax, I'm fine, and I have to take advantage of the good moments."

Dickens must have decided he was off duty, because he dashed to my side again. When we entered the library, he got an enthusiastic welcome.

Claire joked Dickens could give us his paw of approval if our writing was worthy and then brought the group to order. "I can't tell you what it means to me to be surrounded by this group of dedicated writers. The tragic circumstances could have stopped you in your tracks, but you didn't let that happen. I thank you for that."

She glanced toward the door. "When I heard that Issa intended to carry on with her Writer-in-Residence role, I must admit I expected she would change her mind. Much to my surprise and delight, she proved me wrong. She let me know earlier that she's joining us tonight. Her one request is that we not make a fuss, that we let her immerse herself in her role.

"One more thing. Spike O'Malley is joining us too as part of his in-depth article, 'Spotlight on Issa Wright.' Consider him a fly on the wall, not part of our critique group."

Issa came through the door on Spike's arm, and I noticed Brax hovering in the doorway. Only when his mother was settled in a chair did he leave.

Oliver volunteered to go first, and his welcoming words were just the right touch. "I'll take the liberty of speaking for all of us. We may be writers, but words cannot express how sorry we are for your loss."

He looked around the table. "Your presence here tonight is proof positive that you are a consummate professional. Spike, I hope that sentiment makes it into the article. Finally, I'm glad you feel up to joining us, and I know we're all looking forward to your feedback."

Issa ducked her head at his remarks, and we proceeded. Her comments were gracious and professional as we each read our work. Tonight, Dirk was last, and the corners of her mouth lifted as he read aloud his reworked chase scene. "Taking a new direction can be daunting," she said. "That's why I have this quote pasted above my desk at home. 'Be courageous and try to write in a way that scares you a little.' I encourage you to keep at it, Dirk."

She wrapped up by asking Claire to make copies of our writing for her. Promising to provide more in-depth comments in tomorrow's coaching sessions, she made one more request. "Please come prepared to tell me your biggest concern about your writing and the one thing you want to accomplish before you leave. Tomorrow is about confidence. Trust me, all writers, no matter how many books they've published, have moments when they look at their work and think, 'What garbage!' It's natural, and we need to address it."

When she asked me to stay behind, I moved to the chair next to her so Dickens could lie between us. "Leta, thank you for sharing Dickens. He anticipates my every move. I swear he knows before I do that I'm about to cry, and he puts his head in my lap. If he could, I'm sure he'd bring me a tissue. We haven't had a dog or a cat in years, and I'd forgotten how intuitive they are."

She frowned. "That was Trevor's doing. Too much trouble, he said, and I didn't have the energy to argue about it. I won't miss the disagreements, but I'll miss him."

When Dickens nudged her hand, she reached into her pocket for a tissue. "I told you. He knows." After dabbing at her eyes, she studied me. "Belle tells me you and Dave are only recently engaged, and that you're a widow."

"Yes. Henry died several years ago in a cycling accident. I was there, and I'll never forget it. Nothing prepares you for a sudden death like that, so I have a sense of what you're dealing with. There's no way I could have done what you did tonight—sit in a group of people and hold it together. You were calm and composed. I don't know how you did it."

"How long were you married, Leta?"

"Twenty years."

"That may be the difference. Trevor and I were married forty-three years, long enough to pass through the honeymoon stage. Long enough for me to have moments when I didn't think I could bear to live with him. When I wanted him to disappear. Did you ever have moments like that with Henry?"

I was sure my horror came through in my tone. "No. Never. I may not have been in the giddy throes of young love, but I loved Henry with all my being."

"I'm glad for you, Leta. I loved Trevor, but he was an unhappy man, often miserable, rarely joyous. His moods ruled our lives. I didn't live in fear. I lived in dread that something I said or did would deepen his already dark mood. I'll miss him, but it's the old Trevor I'm grieving for, the one I fell in love with, the one I married. That man has been gone a long time."

All I could think was that she must feel awful. She'd entertained thoughts of life without her husband. They argued. And now he was dead.

My response seemed feeble at best. "I'm fortunate that I have so many happy memories of Henry. Dwelling on those made my grief bearable. I hope you can eventually do the same."

Furrowing her brow, she murmured. "I'm not glad he's dead, but in a way, I'm relieved he's gone."

Stunned into silence, I had no response to her disturbing words. All I could do was grasp her hand and leave Dickens with her.

I took my time getting to the cottage. I needed to shake off

Issa's words. Was I surprised that their marriage wasn't happy? No. Nor was I shocked that she had thoughts of life without him. I'd lived through enough of my friends getting divorced to recognize those emotions, but wishing their partners would disappear wasn't tantamount to killing them off. I heard the song "Wishing and Hoping" in my head. Dusty Springfield, however, was singing about love, something entirely different.

Issa's revelations weren't anything I hadn't already sensed about her marriage, so right or wrong, I decided not to share them with Dave. If it seemed relevant later, I would.

When my eyes popped open at 5:30 a.m., it was still dark. I'd slept fitfully with thoughts of murder swirling through my brain—both real and fictional. "Might as well get up," I grumbled to myself.

Tiptoeing to the kitchen, I switched on the coffee maker and added a log to the fire. That's when I heard a faint meow coming from outside. When it turned into a screech, I opened the door. "Christie, what are you doing out there?"

"What do you think? You locked me out."

I picked her up. "Sorry, princess. I was dead tired and must have thought you were inside." If Dave hadn't heard her either, she must have been out 'til all hours.

"Didn't you miss me in bed? Thank goodness, I had Hagrid to keep me company, and Dirk too. I snuggled in his lap by the fire." Her tone was indignant, not angry, and I surmised she'd enjoyed her night out. She rarely got one of those.

After serving her a puddle of milk and a dab of wet food, I took my coffee to the couch and stared at the notes on the wall. After the critique group, we four had spent an hour comparing notes, but no new insights had surfaced. What we needed was a list of suspects. We'd talked about them but hadn't recorded them. On a blank sheet of paper, I wrote Dave, Brax, Dirk, Spike, Oliver, George, and Duncan. Why had I listed only the men? Was I being sexist? Had Jake done the same for his list? For good measure, I added Nora, Evie, Charlie, and Claire.

Across the bottom of the page, I wrote P. D. James's motives for murder—love, lust, lucre, and loathing. I doubted any of the women felt lust or love for Trevor. Was I once again being sexist to think none of the men did either? And what about Issa?

She told me she loved the old version of her husband. Did she loathe what he'd become, or was she just weary of him? I tried to picture her walking unaccompanied to the cliff in the middle of the night with her cane.

I couldn't see it but added her name, anyway. Maybe she walked there with Trevor. Could it have been an attempt on his part to erase his harsh words with a moonlight stroll? But anger flared up and Issa pushed him? She was fragile. Surely, she would have overbalanced and fallen, too—if not over the cliff, at least on the path.

Christie was washing her paws in front of the fire. Too bad she hadn't been out and about when Trevor fell. "Christie, did you and Hagrid stay out all night?"

"Not all of it. We checked the bushes and the woodpile before we curled up in his bed. Later, we went back out through the cat door and wandered the cliff path. We need a cat door at home, Leta."

"I think not, Christie. Chances are Watson would make himself at home and who knows what other critters." Watson, the handsome cat from the manor house, visited us regularly, but not inside.

Staring at the list of names, I wondered what I was missing. What motives had Jake uncovered beyond lucre and, at a stretch, loathing for Brax? And for Dave? Yes, he was furious with the man, but he certainly didn't loathe him.

A thought stirred in the back of my brain. Somewhere, I'd seen another list of motives for murder, not from an author but on a television series. I couldn't recall the name of the show, but the list included jealousy, revenge, fear, and anger. And those words triggered another take on motives—money, love, revenge, and blackmail. There were overlaps and differences among the three lists.

If this were a fantasy novel, the magic marker in my hand would come to life and match the various motives with the suspects I'd listed. Barring that, maybe Dave would wake up with a brilliant idea. It was time I turned my attention to *The Canine Caper*.

Rereading yesterday's words, I edited them with the critique group's input in mind. The next scene would take Lily to the police station to report her missing dog. Describing the reception Lily got there was easy, and my fingers flew across the keyboard.

It wasn't until Dave said good morning that I realized the time. "Oh my gosh, I'll miss breakfast if I don't get a move on." I gave him a hug and dashed to the shower.

When I walked out dressed and ready to go, he and Christie were having a conversation about her food. "Fluff it," she meowed.

He chuckled and moved the dab of food to the middle of her dish. "Is that good?"

"For now." He rolled his eyes, and I could almost believe he understood her.

As we walked to the large patio, it seemed odd not to have Dickens by my side. I was happy Issa found him such a comfort, but I missed him. "Dave, did you see the notes I made this morning?"

"Yup. I see you've added new motives, and it looks like you've expanded the suspect list rather than narrowed it. And I noticed I have pride of place at the top."

"You, Dirk, and Spike—the three amigos, as Jake calls you."

"You know, it's funny. Yesterday, when Spike and I talked about the murder, he mentioned the fact that we know Jake. He also knows you fancy yourself a sleuth, and he compared you to Agatha Raisin."

"At least he didn't say Miss Marple. I wonder if he overheard Wendy and Oliver talking about our books being based on our cases. Anyway, I hope you didn't let on that we're working on this one."

"I downplayed your experience, Tuppence. But he told me he Googled us both when he was prepping for the workshop. Did you know that the *Astonbury Aha!* has mentioned your exploits?"

"I guess I did, but I never thought of someone researching me. And they're not just my exploits. You're as involved as I am."

"Right. These days I am. Spike asked whether Jake had ruled out George and Charlie and Duncan, expecting me to know. It was easy enough to say that I was hoping Jake would rule me out and hadn't asked about anyone else. It made me realize, though, that we haven't talked about them. It's good you put them on the list."

"Yes. For whatever reason, my mind went straight to the guests, but this morning, the others came to mind. We should consider them too. I wonder why Spike asked about them."

"We were talking detective novels, and he mentioned that the police always look to the family first. He commented that if Trevor were his father, pushing him off a cliff would have been tempting."

"Did you two ace crime reporters come up with any theories of the case?"

"The usual stuff, like the least likely person turning out to be guilty, when it's not the family. Like Trevor forced himself on one of the women, and they did him in. Or that George killed him when he found out he'd attacked Charlie. We even joked that Oliver lured him to the cliff with a fake note inviting him for a rendezvous so he could kill him for whatever it was he said at dinner. Mostly far-fetched nonsense."

My imagination took over. "In a murder mystery, we'd learn that Charlie is Trevor's love child from a past affair or that Chef Duncan was blackmailing Trevor over using one of his recipes in a book. As for family, Issa's not mobile enough to have done it. That only leaves Brax."

Dave came to a dead stop. "Leta, wait! What if it was two people? What if Trevor said something unbelievably hateful that night? What if it was the last straw, and Brax and Issa did it together?"

CHAPTER THIRTEEN

My mouth agape, I wondered why that idea hadn't occurred to me, especially after my talk with Issa. "Oh my gosh, Dave. I should have thought of that."

"Why? I know you're the founder of the Little Old Ladies, but you put me and Belle in charge this time. You're taking a back seat, remember?"

Tugging him to the grassy area behind the patio, I told him what Issa had shared with me. "I thought she was trying to come to grips with her emotions, that she told me because she knew I was a widow. I assumed she felt guilty about her feelings, not that she was guilty of murder."

"Hold on, Leta. What if Issa hadn't confided in you? Would you be playing devil's advocate now instead of agreeing with me?"

He had a good point, but I couldn't stop replaying her words. And Brax? I'd been with him when he saw the body. Was he that good of an actor?

Dave cupped my chin. "What's that word you use? Simmer! We need to let this idea simmer. After all, we still have the Charlie as a love child notion to consider."

We were late enough for breakfast that we had the dining room
to ourselves. I'd been ravenous when we set out, but it was all I
could do to choke down toast with my coffee. Dave, on the other
hand, had no problem wolfing down eggs, pancakes, and bacon.

When Wendy poked her head in the door, her smile turned to
a frown. "What's up with you two? You look as though you've
seen a ghost." She sat down and snagged a piece of my toast.

I was debating what to share when Dave solved the problem. "Keep this under your hat, Wendy, but we've discovered
Trevor was blackmailing George, over what we're not sure. And
we've concluded George accidentally sent him tumbling over the
cliff."

She laughed and played along. "Oh, thank goodness. I was
worried Evie and Nora had snuck out that first night and done
it together."

"Wendy, that's it," I said. "You can have two murderers in the
first Constable James book. How clever."

Thank goodness it was time for our morning class. I knew
Wendy had only dropped the subject because we needed to scur-
ry across the hall. Today's topic was Stellar Settings and how to
transport our readers to a locale with colorful descriptions.

As I listened to Claire, I knew I'd done a decent job of describing the lane where Lily lived, especially the pasture with
the donkeys, but there were other details I could beef up, like
the description of the village green. I was eager to get to work,
even though my thoughts kept drifting to Trevor Tarkington's
murder. It would take a monumental effort for me to focus on
my writing this morning.

Claire concluded the talk and passed out the itinerary for the
day. "This is the schedule for the appointments with Issa here in
the library. We'll depart for the Port Isaac tour at two thirty, and
I have it on good authority that a stop at the ice cream shop is a

must."

I was relieved to see that Wendy was first on the schedule and I was last. With two hours of concentrated writing time under my belt, I should be able to have a focused discussion with Issa. Focused on my writing—not on my suspicions.

"Wendy, if the wind isn't too strong, I'm going to try writing behind the cottage today. Shall we meet for lunch after I'm done with Issa?" She gave me a thumbs-up.

Inside the cottage, the fire was inviting, but I wanted to at least try the patio. With a blanket for my legs, my notes on settings, and my laptop, I made myself comfy in the Adirondack chair. As had become my habit, I started by reading and editing my latest section. Only after that did I tackle the village green and the High Street in the village. What fun to describe the building with the yoga studio at one end and Toby's Tearoom at the other.

I glanced up to see Dave and Belle returning from the cliff side path. They were a study in contrasts. Dave was in running tights and a windbreaker. Belle wore her baby blue cloche, and she had the matching scarf tucked around the neck of her long coat.

"Leta," she said, "you missed a lovely walk." She enthused about the view of the boats in the distance and the sparkling sea and deemed it a marvelous way to clear a foggy brain. "You're just in time for a spot of tea, and I must show you the surprise Issa gave me."

Stopping in midstream would disrupt my train of thought, but Belle was hard to resist. "I can spare a few minutes, Belle, but I'll have to get back to work right away."

Dave pecked me on the cheek. "Take your time, sweetheart. We're not going anywhere. I'm researching Dirk and Spike on-line, and Belle's dying to settle in to read her surprise from Issa."

"Thanks. If the words continue to flow, I may join you in an hour. If not, it may be sooner."

Staring at the computer, I reread the last paragraph. I needed to add the stone bridge over the River Elfe and Christmas lights already up on the High Street. It was a joy to describe the festive vibe of Astonbury, though I would give my fictional village a different name.

My fingers were flying across the keyboard when Dave called my name and waved a piece of paper in front of my nose. "Leta, you've got to see this."

I saw a pink Post-it note on a page. It read, "For Belle." When I lifted it, I saw Chapter One in all caps. Below that was what I took to be a newspaper headline.

Playwright Harrison Pope Missing in Snowstorm | Boston Globe

Puzzled, I looked up. "Who's Harrison Pope?"

"Keep going."

Will no one rid me of this troublesome husband? Had I meant those words when I howled them in the dark depths of the forest? After he'd overturned his chair and thrown his wineglass against the kitchen wall, a harbinger of another drunken rage?

When I crept back hours later, the snow was falling fast and thick. I prayed he'd passed out, but the car was gone, and the door stood open to the frosty night air. Where was he?

The first line was a takeoff on Henry II's words about Thomas Becket, though the newspaper headline was contemporary.

"Where did you get this?"

"Come inside. You have to see."

Sitting on Belle's lap, Christie was engaged in one of her favorite activities, chewing on page corners. Given the thick stack of papers Belle held, she'd be happy for quite some time.

Afraid I knew the answer to my question, I queried Belle. "What do you have there?"

She beamed. "Can you believe it? Issa gave me a draft copy

of the book she's working on. No one besides Brax has seen it. I have to give it back, but I'm chuffed beyond words that she's letting me read it. I don't think she'll mind if Christie chews on it." She held up the pages stacked beside her on the couch. "I've read this far already. I know you're busy, but if you want to read this first bit, feel free. "

"Do you think Issa would mind?"

Belle's hand flew to her mouth. "Oh my. I didn't think of that. She was so kind. When she saw me reading *Flames of Fall*, she told me it was her sister Patricia's favorite. She was the person who read early drafts of Issa's books back when she typed them herself. So much sorrow for one person to bear. Her sister died last year, and now she's lost her husband. And because she can no longer type, she dictates her books for Brax to type."

Issa's entire life had changed. "Oh my goodness. What an adjustment that must be to go from typing to dictating. I can barely imagine dictating my short columns, much less an entire book."

"Talking about her sister gave her the idea to let me read this one. She's concerned it's darker than her earlier books. Knowing I'm a huge fan, she wondered if I'd be willing to give her my reaction. I couldn't believe she wanted my opinion, but I'm tickled she asked."

Words failed me. Would Issa have written that first line if she planned to kill her husband? Would she have shared the draft with Belle if she had pushed him to his death? I didn't know what to think. Authors freely admit that they use things they've experienced as fodder for their books. But Trevor had to be very much alive when she wrote these words.

"Belle, have you gotten far enough along to know what happens to the husband?"

"No. The chapters move back and forth in time and the one

I'm reading now is 'Young Love.' It's quite different from her other books in that regard."

When I glanced at Dave, he answered my unspoken question. "I haven't told her."

"Told me what?"

Dave launched into his theory. "Belle, in crime dramas, family members are the first suspects. When you consider how badly Trevor treated both Issa and Brax, they both make sense as suspects, but Issa couldn't have done it on her own. They would have to be in it together."

Belle looked aghast as he warmed to his idea. "I can see it now. Brax types Issa's drafts, and he knows that line, 'Will no one rid me of this troublesome husband?' That night in the cottage, the family has a vicious argument. Trevor even goes to Brax's room to continue berating him. It's the straw that breaks the camel's back."

Following his logic, I played out the scene. "Brax either lures his father or follows him to the cliff, thinking that killing Trevor would free both him and his mother from the escalating emotional abuse. And he pushes him. I can see Issa's words as the trigger, but it's Brax who pulls it."

Belle sat speechless for what seemed like an eternity. "I . . . I don't know what to think. You said 'in it together,' but Issa is writing a book. It's fiction. It's obvious that Brax is more attached to Issa than he was to his father. But does that mean he'd kill him?"

It was her turn to play it out. "If Trevor physically attacked Issa, of course Brax would come to her defense. But killing him after an attack—brooding over it and going after him—that's unthinkable. Even more so if the argument never turned physical. We only know it was loud enough to be heard by others, nothing more."

"Belle," I said, "would it be believable if Brax and Trevor picked up their argument walking along the cliff, it got out of hand, and Trevor accidentally went over?"

Dave paced in front of the fireplace. "And Brax didn't report the fall because he knew how it would look? That's possible—as possible as him purposely pushing him over, I guess."

When Dave first had his brainstorm, it had seemed like a stroke of genius, but as we talked it through, I was finding it less and less plausible. Even when I thought back to what Issa had shared with me. That she would miss her husband, but she'd miss the man she'd fallen in love with, not the man he'd become.

"I'm sorry. For me, this scenario is getting more and more far-fetched by the minute. I saw Brax and Issa together that morning. Both were poised and calm. And on the cliff side, when Brax saw his father's body, his shock was palpable. He couldn't have been faking it."

Watching Dave's face, I saw a flash of disbelief and a hint of indignation before amusement won out. "So, back to the drawing board, it is."

He suggested that Belle continue reading Issa's manuscript and keep an eye out for anything significant while he carried on with his research. Me? I was free to write until it was time for my coaching session with Issa.

I returned to the patio, but not to write. Instead, I laid out my approach to Issa. I'd get coaching another day if I could. Today, I'd do my part to further our investigation.

CHAPTER FOURTEEN

As THE TIME APPROACHED for my meeting with Issa, I grabbed my notebook and moved to the patio behind the main building. Dirk was there with his aviator shades on and his face upturned to the sun. I thought he was asleep until he greeted me. "Are you next? Oliver's in there now."

"Yes, I'm last. How did your session go?"

"She was encouraging about my taking risks with this book, and I was surprised to hear she was trying something new in her latest novel. Old dogs and new tricks, you know? How 'bout you? Are you ready with the answers she asked for?"

I'd given her questions some thought, but not much. The honest answer as to my biggest concern was that I was clueless about writing fiction. Since I'd committed to co-writing with Wendy, what I wanted to accomplish was to learn the craft and feel more confident. Chanting, "Yes, I can. Yes, I can" hadn't worked so far. I said as much to Dirk.

He threw back his head and laughed. "Issa Wright may be a famous author, but she doesn't have a magic wand. Take it from a man who's written a dozen books, you'll always doubt yourself. And I think what you've shared with us so far has been well done."

"But what do I know about plots? I'm an avid reader who's only written training manuals and stream-of-consciousness newspaper columns. I'll admit I can craft a few paragraphs, but stringing together chapters in a cohesive and suspenseful way takes a lot more than that."

His next words sounded like what Dave kept telling me. "You've got a head start on most would-be writers because of your journalism background. The rest will come." He leaned back again with his face upturned.

How my brain worked was a mystery to me. Dirk's comment about my so-called journalism background led to thoughts of Dave and Spike's career trajectories. Dave continued to write reviews and articles, but he had also published a book and was contemplating another. Did Spike have similar aspirations?

I recalled Dirk's comment about misery loving company. "Dirk, I'm curious. While you and Spike were commiserating the other night, was there any mention of him writing a book? Dave's article on J. M. Barrie became the catalyst for a book. That must happen to other journalists. Something triggers a need to dive deep into a topic, and the result is a book."

His reply was so long in coming, I thought he'd dozed off. "Let me think. It was something about losing."

"What was?"

Dirk lifted his head. "Spike's book. If I'm not mistaken, it's been out a while."

Before I could pursue that news, Oliver opened the patio door. "Leta, I'm fetching a cup of tea for Issa. May I get one for you too?"

Further questions about Spike's book would have to wait. Carrying the two cups of tea Oliver prepared, I pushed open the door to the library. Until Dickens bounded over to greet me, I'd forgotten he was with Issa. He was a welcome sight.

I had expected her to be tired by now. Instead, she looked energized. I could only think the writing discussions were helping.

She had my two earlier pages in front of her. "Shall we start with your opening before moving on to the questions I posed?"

"Issa, I want your input on my writing, but I have a more pressing concern at the moment, and I'd like to address that, if I may?"

Her answer was to turn the pages face down. When I put my hand over the arm of the chair, Dickens got the signal. He came to my side, and I ruffled his ears.

"Issa, you already know that Wendy's and my Constable James books are based on our sleuthing adventures."

"So, I gathered, à la Jessica Fletcher. And I understand from Claire that you were instrumental in clearing her fiancé and working out how her sister died."

"If she told you that, you understand that clearing one suspect means investigating others. That's what I want to speak with you about. For one thing, Dave is high on the suspect list. Like just about everyone on the premises that night, he has no alibi."

At her puzzled look, I explained. "He was up late drinking, and I didn't hear him come in. And because he and Trevor exchanged unpleasantries during the panel, DI Nancarrow thinks Dave has a motive."

"You mean because my husband insulted you and Dave both? Unpleasantries doesn't do it justice, and if that's all it took for someone to attack my husband, there'd be a long list."

"Issa, I don't know any other way to say this. You've engaged two solicitors, so you must know Brax is on the list. And you would be if . . ."

"If not for my Parkinson's."

"Yes. But here's the thing. I read the first page of the manuscript you gave Belle, and remembered what you said last night. I can't help wondering . . ."

She leaned forward, a look of concern on her face. "Leta, what's wrong?"

"What happens to the husband?"

Her eyes grew wide as she sat back in her chair. "Oh, my goodness. Your reaction is exactly what I'm worried about. I mean it wasn't until . . . until Trevor died. Before that, I was only concerned it was too much of a departure from my other books—too dark. I *know* what happens to the husband, but readers won't know until the midpoint."

She rubbed her hands over eyes. "It may be years before I release this book, if ever. My editor may be dead set against it, given Trevor's . . . Trevor's murder. She's been happy with it thus far, but I can hear her gasping now over the damage it could do to my brand in the wake of Trevor's death. I can't believe I've worked on this book for over a year, and it may never see the light of day."

Leaning her head back against the chair, she closed her eyes. "Oh, for goodness' sake, that sounded heartless."

I repeated her words. "A year?"

"Yes. But when my readers see the first line, they're bound to connect it to my . . . to Trevor." She tilted her head. "Unless the description suggests that the storm is a life-changing event rather than a death sentence. The only problem is it ruins the early suspense."

Had she just answered my question? "Issa, does the husband die?"

"No! It's not life imitating art. I didn't have a premonition about Trevor. It's fiction. Yes, if I could have invented a life-changing event for Trevor, I would have. Did I pray that by some miracle, we could start anew and regain at least a small measure of happiness? Yes, but we'll never have the chance now.

"In my book, getting stranded in a snowstorm and thinking he'll die is the husband's life-changing event. The story is how the couple deals with it. Has the wife grown so timid and withdrawn that she's unable to adjust to her husband becoming the man she once loved? Whether they can change enough to be happy together is the central question. And for the record, I may have learned to keep Trevor at a distance, but no one has ever called me timid."

This was why she was a master storyteller—why she was an award-winning author. How much of her life had she channeled into her novels?

"In real life, the central question is when will the police arrest the person who murdered my husband. I didn't realize Dave was a suspect, but I'm certainly aware they're looking at my son. Ridiculous. You don't kill your father because you argued with him."

"Issa, you only have to read the papers to know that scenario is more common than you think. I trust DI Nancarrow to find the killer, but I know he has to be sure about Brax first—not to mention Dave."

"What can I do? Would seeing Trevor's hate mail help uncover motives or suspects?"

"I guess it couldn't hurt. But what are the chances he received hate mail from someone anywhere near here? If there's evidence that a guest at this workshop sent him some, wouldn't Brax have already told DI Nancarrow that?"

Issa leaned forward. "He mentioned the records to the detective, but he seemed uninterested. Brax has them in an online folder and keeps a spreadsheet of them too. Personally, I think he reads too many books where victims get old-fashioned threats with pasted letters from magazines. Nowadays, everything is online and traceable. Still, his spreadsheet might come in handy."

If Jake thought it was too much of a long shot to spend man-power on, maybe it was. But that didn't mean that three little old ladies and an old codger couldn't give it a look. *Face it,* I thought, *it's time for you to take an active role in this case. So much for writing.*

"Okay, Issa, I'm on it."

As I stood to leave, Issa stopped me. "But wait, Leta, what about your writing? I've made notes."

"Not now. Lily and her missing dog will have to wait for another day."

CHAPTER FIFTEEN

HURRYING OUT THE BACK door, I stopped short when I spied Dirk still relaxing in the rare bit of sunshine. If I was going to look at a hate mail spreadsheet, there was one more thing I needed to know from him. "Dirk, excuse me, I'm curious. In thinking about the pen name Wendy and I made up for ourselves, I wondered how close yours was to your real name." A lie, but a harmless one.

"Not close at all. I used my real name, Patrick Owens, for my WWII fiction, but I think Dirk Blackthorne has a thriller vibe, don't you?"

"Heck, Dirk, the name would work for a thriller character. Maybe you could pull an Anthony Horowitz move and make yourself a character in one of your books." In his Hawthorne and Horowitz series, the writer partners with a detective to solve murder mysteries.

He gave me a thumbs-up as I left him. I had two names to look for so far—Patrick Owens and Spike O'Malley. This talk of pen names made me wonder whether Oliver, Evie, and Nora had used pen names. Oliver had mentioned using something for his traditional romance books, but romance books were so often treated as lesser works, I couldn't imagine Trevor Tarkington reviewing one.

On our small patio, Spike was giving Dave casting lessons. "Look at him, Leta. I may make a fisherman of him yet."

Christie meowed from her perch on the Adirondack chair. "So far, all he's done is tangle himself in the line. Do they really catch fish with those things?"

"Are you two planning an outing?"

Instead of a yes or no answer, I got an involved explanation of tide tables, wind, and whatnot. "If I can interrupt this fascinating discussion for one moment, I have a question. Spike, I just learned that you're an author. How did we not know this?"

"Bloody hell. Hardly anyone knows, and I'd prefer to keep it that way. My stab at writing fiction was an abysmal failure, and the fewer people who know the better." When he drew back and cast again, I took the hint.

I put the kettle on, and before long, Dave joined me. "How did your coaching session go?"

"Well, about that. Coaching is on the back burner for now."

"Does that mean what I think it does, Tuppence? Have you been snooping?"

"Yes. Think about it, Dave. The first forty-eight hours of an investigation are crucial, and as far as I can tell, Jake is making very little progress. He needs us."

He tried unsuccessfully to hide his smile. "I wondered how long you'd be able to hold out. No matter your resolution to write murder mysteries rather than solve them, I knew it was only a matter of time. I kept hoping Jake would hurry up and make an arrest before you succumbed to temptation, but no joy there."

"Have you been feeding him our info? I just heard from Issa that Brax has a file on Trevor's hate mail, but Jake hasn't pursued it."

"It's Belle who's been speaking with Jake. He's done his best to confine our conversations to my memories of our first night here and of my finding the body. I don't honestly think he still sees me as a suspect, but he hasn't said differently."

"It's possible he was inclined to be collaborative when Wendy and I fed him information in Tintagel because we weren't suspects. We were his highly intelligent eyes and ears, not to mention research assistants."

Dave cracked up. "Is that what you call it? Why don't you get him over here to see what we've come up with so far? Spike thought it was quite impressive."

"Spike? You let Spike see our notes? Was that wise?"

"What was I supposed to do when he knocked on the door? Shoo him away? He surprised me with a book on coastal fishing plus the loan of a rod and reel. We eventually made it to the patio to practice, but not before he noticed our unique wallpaper. He was especially taken with the four Ls, and we compared notes from our crime reporting days."

All I could do was shake my head. "What did he have to say about his name on the suspect list? "

"That he was in good company." Dave squinted. "It jogged his memory, though. He remembered that after I left that night, it wasn't long before Dirk called it quits too. Spike thought he was the last man standing until Brax came in looking for wine. He offered him whiskey, but Brax isn't a whiskey drinker."

"Brax? What time was that?"

"I asked, but Spike's memory is as foggy as mine. He doesn't recall when I left or when he went to bed, much less about Dirk or Brax."

We desperately needed a firm timeline, with the comings and goings of the three amigos, Brax dropping by, Oliver overhearing Brax and Trevor, and Dirk encountering Trevor in the hallway.

We had data points, but not times. Did Jake have one? And did he know precisely when Trevor died?

"Did Spike have any other comments?"

"Nothing we didn't already know. He read over the list of suspects and saw that we'd added the locals, and he noted that the revenge motive would fit for Dirk before he shifted to writing thrillers. Oh! And he mentioned lucre as a motive for Brax and Issa, as they surely stand to inherit. To me, though, lucre doesn't fit with a spur-of-the-moment murder. Boy, that sounds cold—spur-of-the-moment murder."

"Dave, what do you think about grabbing lunch and bringing it back here? I need to mull over what I heard today and add more notes. But, for heaven's sake, we can't allow suspects in here! Except for you, that is."

At least he chuckled at that. "Got it. I'll get lunch. Shall I invite Belle and Wendy to join us?"

"I think not. I'll text Wendy to tell her I'm in pondering mode, and we'll catch them up later."

Studying the pages scattered around the room, I jotted my notes on one of the blank ones. Spike's book, Dirk's real name, Trevor's hate mail, Spike seeing Brax the night of the murder. There was plenty of new info to sift through.

I taped two pieces of sketchpad paper together with the short sides attached and hung the combo on the wall. When hung sideways, it gave me a piece suitable for a timeline. Across the bottom, I captured bullet points.

- Spike and Dave drink in the library

- They bump into Dirk

- He drinks with them in the front room

  ○ Oliver overhears Brax and Trevor

- ○ Dirk gets a bottle from his room and encounters Trevor in the hallway (Immediately after Oliver overhears the argument?)

- • Dave is the first to leave

- • Dirk is next

- • Brax shows up—from where?

  - ○ Does he stay?

  - ○ If so, who leaves first—Spike or Brax?

It was tempting to make assumptions about the order, but the adage about the word 'assume' stopped me. I needed facts, and if Belle was still next door, that was a good place to start.

When I knocked, I discovered Belle was alone. "Yes, it's just me. Brax went to have lunch with his mum, and I told Wendy I wasn't hungry. I'm too engrossed in this book to stop now. And I've been nibbling most of the morning."

"May I get you to answer a few quick questions, Belle? I understand you're the conduit to Jake. How easy is it for you to recall what you've shared with him? And what he's told you, if anything?"

Belle realized right away that I was now on the case full-time. "Thank goodness, you've got your priorities straight, luv. This case needs your skills. And Wendy's too. As for Jake, he's been more tight-lipped than he has in the past."

"What have you told him about our findings? Has he seen any of it as helpful?"

"Not that he's let on. I told him straightaway what all Brax did for his mum and dad, and his reaction was a nod. Mentioned the hate mail, too, and he mumbled something about that not being much of a surprise. I don't know what's going on with him."

"Is he keeping his distance from our investigation because Dave is a suspect?" I was thinking aloud. "No, that can't be it. He knows full well Dave didn't throw Trevor over the cliff. Wendy and I may have to skip the trip to Port Isaac and find Jake instead."

Belle laughed. "I'll be happy to tell you all about Port Isaac. Dave says I must try the ice cream, and I can't wait to see the sights from *Doc Martin*. After missing the trip to Fowey, I'm determined to make this one."

Seeing Dave walk by, I pecked Belle on the cheek and left her to her reading. Today's meal was fish and chips, not something I often indulged in, but passing on fish when in Cornwall seemed like a sin. I suggested we take a brief break and enjoy our lunch before getting down to business.

Dave raved about the fish and wondered why it wasn't quite as good at the Ploughman in Astonbury. "Leta, if I'm any good at catching fish, could you fry them?"

"You're out of luck. You'd think as a Southern girl, I could at least fry chicken, but I can't. When I try, the coating always sticks to the pan. I'm told it's because I don't get the grease hot enough."

"I bet you could bake or broil it, though. I can see myself fishing in the River Elfe at home, once I get more tips from Spike."

An image of Henry flashed into my brain. "Oh my goodness, Dave. Henry once tried to teach me to fly fish. You should have seen us. We stood in a meadow with me attempting to cast. I was so unbelievably awful that Henry gave up. That was fine by me because I never wanted to fish in the first place. I much preferred to sit in a lawn chair and read while he fished."

As I cleared the kitchen table, Dave perused the additions to the wallpaper scheme. "I should have known Dirk Blackthorne was a pen name, just never thought about it." He studied it further without comment before turning to me. "There's got to be a way to at least guesstimate times. How 'bout Oliver? I doubt he was in his cups like the rest of us. Maybe he can be more definitive."

"In his cups! I don't think I've ever heard anyone say that. I've only read it."

He was Googling the origins of the phrase when a call came in from Wendy. "Shall I meet you at the bus?"

"No. I'm debating going to Truro to confront Jake."

"You're what? I know we've been picking up things here and there, but I thought Mum and Dave were handling the active part of the investigation."

With a groan, I confessed. "I can't help myself. I'm stepping in. Do you want to join me?"

"I wish I could, but Mum is looking forward to us doing the *Doc Martin* tour together, and I can't let her down. Is there anything I can do in Port Isaac to move things along?"

What I needed was timing for the night of the murder. I couldn't query the guests while they were touring, but she could.

"Yes. One new thing I've learned is that Spike saw Brax late the night of the murder. Since you and Oliver have become best friends, can you press him to pinpoint the approximate time he overheard Brax and Trevor that first night? New information keeps coming to light, and I'm having the devil of a time mapping it out. I plan to see Brax about hate mail, and I'll also ask about his timeline."

"No problem. I'll handle Oliver. And I heard something interesting from Rhys. When we spoke this morning, he had plenty to say about Snarkington. Did you know the man disliked

Golden Age authors?" Of course, Wendy's boyfriend would know that given his involvement with the Golden Age Literary Association.

I forgot Wendy wasn't here for the panel discussion where Trevor had expressed his opinion on the likes of Agatha Christie and Dorothy Sayers. "Oh yes, he called them stuffy."

"Rhys says he didn't stop there. He's gone after Sophie Hannah for wasting her talent on the Poirot series and Jill Paton Walsh for doing the same with Lord Peter Wimsey. Rhys says the GALA members dubbed him an uncouth gadfly."

The GALAs were ardent supporters of all things Golden Age, so I wasn't surprised they were defensive about the modern-day Christie and Sayers authors. "He was rude and argumentative for sure, but you'll have to tell me what a gadfly is. Isn't it funny how you can see a word all your life, but not know what it means?"

If possible, Wendy was more of a word nerd than I was. "It's any kind of fly that bites cattle, but for us humans, it's someone who criticizes people left and right. Instead of offering criticism constructively, they do it in a way meant to get under your skin. That seems to fit the bill for Trevor Tarkington, doesn't it?"

In my head, I heard the stingers he'd lobbed at Dave. "That pretty much nails it. He must have attacked other British authors, too. I wonder whether there are any in the vicinity of Port Isaac. What if our suspect list is broader than we think and there's a local author we should consider?" Wendy promised to check with Rhys to see if he knew of any off the top of his head.

"Found it," Dave said, as I hung up. "In his cups may have come from the Bible or seventeenth century England. And Washington Irving used it in 'The Legend of Sleepy Hollow' in 1820."

I responded with a recap of my gadfly discussion with Wendy. "Instead of two peas in a pod, Dave, we're two easily distracted word nerds. Beyond asking Rhys for help, how can we find out whether Trevor Tarkington wrote scathing reviews about any authors who live in Cornwall?"

"The hate mail data would be a place to start. And Claire may have researched local authors when she was planning this workshop. She'll be on the tour this afternoon, but I can ask when she gets back. Do you want me to tackle Brax and Claire?"

"Yes. I'm going to track down Jake and make him talk to me. Who knows? If he doesn't plan to visit here today, I may be forced to drive to Truro and beard the lion in his den."

Dave snapped photos of my notes and made additional notes on his phone. "In addition to the hate mail, I've got a list of questions for Brax, like who left first that night, him or Spike? What time was it? When did his father visit his room? I bet Jake already has those answers, but they'll help us, regardless. You gave me Dirk's real name, but did you by chance, get the name of his book about his grandmother?"

"No. Which reminds me, did Spike say anything else about his book after I left you two out back? I can't believe he's so tight-lipped about it."

"It was obvious he didn't want to discuss it, so I wanted to Google it before I asked him anything more about it. It's odd. I didn't find anything by Spike O'Malley except for articles. He surprised me when he said it was fiction, though there are several renowned journalists who successfully made that shift. Not only Hemingway, but also writers like Hunter S. Thompson, Joan Didion, and Tom Wolfe. Heck, even George Orwell was a journalist first."

"One more thing for your list this afternoon—talk to Spike."

As he headed for the door, he tossed off a comment. "You know, Tuppence, that conversation may require another trip to the ice cream shop."

"Right, with your focus on ice cream and fishing, we'll have the case wrapped up in no time!"

CHAPTER SIXTEEN

I STUDIED WHAT I had jotted across the bottom of the timeline page and called Wendy. After giving her an assignment, I hurried next door to find Brax. In the distance, I saw Spike and Dave chatting near the main building.

Brax answered the door. "Hi, Leta, are you looking for Mom?"

"Nope. It's you I came to see."

When I explained I was in full-on detective mode and had questions for him, he stepped outside. "I've already told DI Nancarrow what I know—to no avail, mind you—but if you think it will help, have at it."

"Brax, I don't want to overpromise, but we three little old ladies and our clueless old codger have gotten to the bottom of a few cases that stymied the police. Dave will drop by later to look at your hate mail records, and I only have two quick questions for you. One, that first night, when you went looking for a late-night glass of wine, who left the front room first—you or Spike?"

He crossed his arms. "So, when you told me before that you were 'close' to a few investigations, you were what—downplaying your role? I knew something wasn't quite right about your explanation. Anyway, it was me who left first. Why does it matter?"

"It may not, but mapping out a timeline helps me see things more clearly. Okay, next question. I'm sure you answered this for Jake Nancarrow, but when was the last time you saw your dad?"

"Sometime between eleven and twelve Saturday night. I'd just gotten Karen, my girlfriend, on the phone, and I had to hang up when Dad pounded on the door."

That was helpful. That meant someone could corroborate his story. "Did you have a chance to call her back?"

"Yes. Sharing the blow-by-blow of the evening with her helped me settle down and get to sleep. I spoke with her for nearly an hour. Things looked brighter the next morning—at least until, you know."

"What time did you call her, Brax?" I wondered whether Jake had been able to narrow down the time of death enough that the call and the emails would clear Brax.

He pulled out his phone. "Look. It was one here. I caught her after her evening run in Boston. We talked while she did her stretching routine." He chuckled. "She's much more fit than I am. In fact, she left early the next day on a weeklong cycling and camping trip to Maine with two girlfriends."

I pictured myself adding the information to the horizontal page on my cottage wall. "Thanks, Brax. You know, Dirk bumped into your dad when he was leaving your room, but he couldn't pinpoint the time. If you and Dave can locate anything meaningful in the hate mail records, that will help."

"I see you're also owning up to the clueless old codger being a detective. Who else— Wendy, Belle? I'm willing to work with anyone to find Dad's killer."

I explained we were a team. "Later, I'll show you our process. At the moment, Dave is on records detail. I have other fish to fry."

"Records I can do, Leta. You have no idea how organized I am—boringly organized, as Dad would put it. Before I went to work for Mom and Dad, they had a string of personal assistants, each with their own way of handling things. When I came on board, I went back years to document everything. I did that for both Mom and Dad, but since Dad was more prolific—in not only books but also mail—his was the larger task. I've got every review Dad ever wrote, his correspondence, his podcast guests, and interviews others did with him. It's all in the cloud."

"Speaking of the cloud, have you had any success locating your father's book with the new ending?"

"No. The last version I can find is dated July, and that's the one his editor has. But I haven't given up. I contacted our housekeeper in Boston, and she's going to search Dad's office. He has an old desktop computer in there connected to a large screen. Maybe there's something on it. It makes no sense that he wouldn't have touched the book in several months."

In our cottage, I was adding notes to the timeline when my phone pinged with a text from Wendy.

"Oliver in bed at 10:30, so overheard Trevor & Brax before that. Dirk says 11:30ish."

My partner in crime had come through on her assignment. Trevor had visited his son twice that night, and the information from Oliver and Dirk confirmed what Brax had told me. I'd had it in my head that Oliver overheard the father and son argument right before Dirk encountered Trevor in the hallway. Instead, they were two different instances.

It didn't matter unless there was a reason Brax only mentioned the later time. That's when it hit me. He answered what I asked. The last time he saw his dad. I was going to have to do a better job of phrasing questions if I wanted to solve this case.

Next up was tracking down Jake. I caught him in his car. "Leta, I thought you were writing. Oh wait, I bet you called to pick my brain on some arcane element of British law."

"Very funny, Jake. I called because I've given up writing until Dave is in the clear."

"And if I told you he was, would you go back to plotting your Constable James mystery?"

"Are you serious? Why don't we know that?"

A chuckle came down the line. "Because I'm on my way there and thought I'd tell you two in person."

"Beside the fact you knew all along he didn't do it, how did you clear him?"

"Would you believe one of the women in Sycamore Cottage heard meowing and got up to check on the cat? She witnessed Dave being escorted to your door round about midnight by two cats, not just one. She waited until he got inside because she was worried he'd fall. I can't believe he didn't wake you up."

"It's odd. I was vaguely aware he came to bed, just not what time. Not to look a gift horse in the mouth, but how do you know he didn't sneak back out?"

"According to Evie, I think it was, he could barely stand. If he'd made it as far as the cliff in his condition, it might have been him at the bottom of it, instead of Trevor Tarkington."

I shuddered. "Don't even joke about that. What about your prime suspect? Are you any closer to clearing Brax?"

"I'm headed your way." His next few words were garbled.

"Jake, are you there?"

"Bloody hell! I've got to handle this mess. Some gormless git is stopped in the middle of the road. Should be about thirty minutes."

If I were going to sit down with Jake and get him to listen to me, I needed to have my ducks in a row. He was a patient man—much more so than his girlfriend Gemma, the DI in Astonbury—but he had his limits.

I knew I was nowhere near as organized as I usually was in these circumstances. Was it possible the experts were right—that multitasking was inefficient? But if that were the case, how had I identified a killer just last month, despite being neck-deep in facilitating a team building event?

Could it be that the act of writing consumed more brainpower? For me, imagining thoughts and actions for a fictional character, even based on someone I knew, required near-total immersion in the story. It demanded every ounce of my attention, leaving little room for pondering the Trevor Tarkington case. It was time to focus on only one thing.

I studied the pages on the wall and started a fresh page of notes. Next, I closed my eyes and replayed what happened Sunday—from the moment Dave came running toward me on the patio.

- In the front room of the inn, I saw Charlie, Dirk, and Brax.

- We jogged to the cliff, and Brax identified his dad by his blue jacket.

- I saw a glint of something in the bracken.

- An empty bottle of whiskey sat on the counter in the Tarkington cottage.

Think, Leta. What is it about whiskey? Claire poured whiskey for Spike and Dave in the library. They carried the bottle to the front room and carried on drinking, so much so that Dirk had to get another bottle from his room. Good grief! Did they finish a second bottle?

Charlie or George should know the answer to my question. Leaving the cottage, I nearly tripped over Christie, lying belly up on the walkway. "Well, don't you look comfy?"

She rolled and stretched. "Do you have treats? I need a treat." When I shook my head, she meowed, "Maybe Hagrid will share his."

In front of the main building, George was sweeping the stone walk. "George, I need your help. Who cleans the main rooms in the mornings, you or Charlie?"

He gave me a bemused look before answering. "Charlie does, while I cook breakfast."

"Is she around now?" He directed me to the kitchen where Charlie was prepping hors d'oeuvres for later.

I was sure I sounded like a madwoman when I dove right in. "Charlie, on Sunday morning, the day we found Trevor Tarkington, can you recall what all was in the front room when you cleaned it?"

With a puzzled look, she ticked items off on her fingers. "Yes, I'd cleared the room after the panel discussion and hadn't really expected to find much after that. But there were several dirty tumblers, an empty whiskey bottle, and one of our large cans of nuts." She put her hands on her hips. "I'm sure it was Spike who helped himself to that."

"Why Spike?"

"When he dated my sister, he helped out around here, so he knows where everything is. He's still a bottomless pit."

She must have noticed my look of surprise. "We attended Wadebridge School, but I was five years younger than them. You know, the pesky little sister who followed them everywhere. Duncan still teases me about it."

"I remember now. Spike said he was from around here. And Duncan? Did he go to school with you too?"

"Yes, it's a small world here on the coast. We both remember him from before he was Spike O'Malley the reporter. Duncan and I are the same age and have always been mates. After culinary school, he came back and married his sweetheart from Wade-bridge. It's about fifty-fifty. Half of the ones who leave never return."

Storing that nugget away, I got down to business. "Did you happen to find a second bottle of whiskey, perhaps half empty?"

"No, and I'm sure, because I searched for one when I found two dirty tumblers on a table out back. If there hadn't been a bottle top beneath the table, I would have thought someone poured drinks inside before wandering to the patio. I didn't find a second bottle, though, so I don't know what the cap went to."

Christie meowed. "I bet Hagrid knows. He came back here after I went inside that night, with Dave."

I filed that info away for later. "Any chance you remember an empty whiskey bottle in Dirk's trash?"

"Wasn't one. I know because I separate the rubbish for recy-cling. No whiskey bottles in any of the bedrooms or cottages except for the one on the counter in the Tarkingtons' cottage. Macallan's, if I recall." She chuckled. "What's this all about? Are you the rubbish warden?"

"If only it were that simple. No. I'm trying to map out who was where that night, and a second whiskey bottle might have given me an answer. Thanks for your help. I'll let you get back to work."

If the second bottle wasn't on the premises, inside or outside, it had to be the bottle Jake found on the cliff path. But how did it get there? And which two guests sat at the table drinking? Fingerprints would have provided an answer, but the glasses had been washed and put away by the time Jake arrived.

Christie and I left via the back patio. "Christie, can you ask

Hagrid what he saw Saturday night? If he knows who was drinking out here, that would help."

Meowing, she peeled off around the inn. With any luck, Hagrid would provide a vital clue. I texted Wendy with another task,
to ask Dirk if the three amigos finished his bottle of whiskey, too.
Bottom line, I needed to know when he last saw it, empty or not.
Oh! And what brand it was. I suggested she use a gift for Rhys
as a cover story.

By the time Jake knocked on my door, I'd added notes to the
timeline and was deep in thought. For whatever reason, I kept
coming back to Dirk and Spike as the likeliest suspects. If only I
could articulate why. In all the best mystery books, the detectives
didn't rely on intuition or gut instinct. They had clues to follow.

"Hello there, Leta. Have you cracked the case yet?"

"No. I've asked questions and have new info, at least new to
me, but I don't know how helpful it is. Now, what can you tell
me about Brax? That you've cleared him, right?"

He tossed his jacket on a chair. "Any chance of a cup of tea,
first?"

"Sure thing. Coming right up."

As I put the kettle on, he moved around the room, reading the
pages stuck to the wall. "This looks like my whiteboard at the
station, except for this."

He pointed to the two recent pages. "I know about Brax
encountering Spike late Saturday night, but what's this about
someone named Patrick Owens?"

That he was avoiding my question about Brax was an answer
in itself, but I played along. "You know that Trevor Tarkington
was a thoroughly unlikeable person, right? Dirk was open with
me about getting an awful review from him on his first book."

"But who is Patrick Owens? Tell me I haven't missed a guest."

"No. That's Dirk's real name and the one he used for his

first books." I explained the book was historical fiction based on Dirk's grandmother, and that Trevor had panned it.

"Ouch, that must have stung. Had the two met before this event?"

"Not that I know of, and Dirk was trying to avoid a meeting. That's why he skipped dinner and the panel discussion on Saturday. Did he tell you they bumped into each other in the hall that night?"

"Yes. I asked everyone when they last saw the victim, so I've got that." He sipped the cup of tea I handed him. "Let me guess. You're going to tell me there was more to it, right?"

"It's always nice when I dig up something you don't already know. Tarkington managed to live up to his nickname of Snarkington with a snide remark. I can only think that the man researched the participants before he got here because he knew Dirk was Patrick. So, it was salt in the wound for Dirk, and a possible motive."

"Not much of one, but as good as what I had for Dave."

"That's exactly what I said."

"I sense you haven't quite forgiven me for putting Dave on the suspect list."

Hands on my hips, I snapped back. "What was your first clue? Tell me, did you really think he could have done it?"

"Of course, I didn't, but I had to be thorough, and I hoped it would serve another purpose. If the others thought Dave was a suspect, they might let their guard down. Except that didn't happen. Now, I also see a note about Spike and a book. I thought he was a journalist."

I explained I'd discovered Spike was also an author, but that he'd shut me down when I asked about his book, and that Dave had been unable to find it online anywhere. "Dave plans to pursue it with him. I saw them talking earlier so he may have an answer by now. I only knew because Dirk mentioned it."

"Help me out here, Leta. Why does it matter?"

"It may be a stretch, but it made me think that Tarkington may have given Spike's book an ugly review."

"And the rest of the authors in attendance—did the victim trash their books, too?"

"Not that anyone's mentioned. I haven't directly asked, but I can't imagine him taking the time to review a romance novel. The genre is hugely popular with readers but openly dissed by authors who write anything else. Claire could tell you more about that bias. Anyway, that's why I didn't ask Oliver or Evie or Nora."

A thought struck me. "Though it's worth mentioning that Trevor insulted Oliver Saturday night at dinner. I don't know the exact words, just that Evie labeled it a homophobic remark."

"Oh, I got that alright. The same way I heard about the insults lobbed at Dave. People were quite forthcoming about all that. It's the one-on-one conversations they keep close to the chest—like your friend Dirk, for example. I asked him when he last saw the victim, and he said he passed him in the hall around 11:30, not that he spoke with him."

He gave me an admiring look. "I get why Gemma calls you a Nosey Parker, but it still amuses me how irritating she finds it when you bring her useful bits like this. If you lived here, I'd put you on retainer. Or I'd get you to teach a class on your interview technique."

I tried not to beam. "You know it's partially that I'm not with the police. The rest of it comes from working in Human Resources all those years. I'm not sure it's something I could teach—other than asking open-ended questions."

"Whatever it is, it works." He pointed to the line item about Spike and Brax. "I know they connected late Saturday night. Are you going to tell me their whole conversation, too?"

With a laugh, I told him there was nothing to report there. "I have something that might be significant, but first I want to know where you are on Brax. He told me he was on the phone with his girlfriend. Doesn't that give him an alibi?"

He brushed his auburn hair from his forehead. "Once I catch up with his girlfriend in the States, the alibi may be solid. He claims she's off in the wilds of Maine with poor reception, and that's why I can't get her. I can confirm he dialed her number, and it appears they were on the phone for an hour. But it's suspicious that's she's conveniently unavailable. If he wanted to set up an alibi, he could have used a call duration app to fake it."

"Are you kidding me? What the heck is that?"

"You download it from an app store, and it allows you to set up a fake call with whatever caller ID you want, like a girlfriend's. And you can make it look like either an outgoing or incoming call for however long you want it to last."

"But Jake, that would mean he planned to kill his father, that this was a premeditated murder. And the girlfriend would have to be in on it, right? I find that hard to believe."

"Why? He's clearly attached to his mother, and he makes no bones about he and his father not getting along. Based on the various overheard conversations and what Brax intimated to me, his dad was beastly. I'd even venture that he mistreated his wife—not physically but emotionally. I haven't gotten my hands on the will yet, but it's likely that Brax and his mother stand to inherit. That's motive enough for me."

Given that I'd considered much the same scenario and added collusion between Brax and Issa, Jake's idea should sound reasonable to me. But I'd spoken with Issa. She'd confided in me, and I believed her. This wasn't a mystery novel or a Shakespearean play. I still couldn't see Brax going off into the night to rid his mother of her obnoxious husband. Both he and Issa would have to be Oscar-worthy actors to fake their shock, much less plan a techno alibi involving an app and a girlfriend. Talk about the stuff of fiction!

"There's also the fact that the only three with an alibi are Evie, Nora, and the chef. Everyone else was on their own—even you."

"I knew about Evie and Nora, but what's Chef Duncan's alibi?"

"Drove home to Padstow to his wife and two kids. And I know that his wife could be alibiing him even if he wasn't there, but I'm going with it for now. Even if he'd spent the night, what motive would he have for killing Tarkington? If the weapon had been a kitchen knife, I might take another look."

"I have no reason to suspect him, but are you aware that he knows both Charlie and Spike?"

He groaned. "No. I missed that bit of history. Do you have a conspiracy theory in mind?"

"Very funny, Jake. Of course not, but you asked me to let you know what I came across, and that fact cropped up."

I made sure my next words dripped with sarcasm. "Since you don't want to know about Chef Duncan marrying his high school sweetheart, can we talk about Brax? I was with him when we found his father, and he was genuinely shocked. That's why I'm not convinced."

When Jake opened his mouth to interrupt me, I cut him off. "Let's look at motive more closely. Love, lust, lucre, loathing, or revenge—I admit you could posit lucre as a motive for both Brax and Issa. Perhaps even loathing, though Issa tells me she loved Trevor despite his behavior. As close as Brax is to her, would he kill the man she loved?"

Jake's only response was to roll his eyes, a look that made me think of Gemma. That was her trademark reaction to anything

I suggested when I stuck my nose into her cases.

"Hear me out. There's no evidence of love or lust that I can find, and what revenge could Brax or Issa want? That's why I've put Dirk and Spike at the top of my list, instead. Dirk has reason to loath him because the man labeled the tale of his grandmother's life as a resistance fighter a fantasy. Never mind dashing Dirk's hopes of making a name in historical fiction, the review made it sound as though his grandmother made it all up or, at best, greatly exaggerated her life. Yes, Dirk's done well with his thrillers, but his first love is World War II fiction, and you can't discount how Trevor hurt the grandmother. Loathing leading to revenge makes sense to me."

"I had the impression you liked Dirk."

"I do, but that doesn't mean he didn't fly off the handle after drinking all night or worse, arrive here with revenge in mind. He could be a cool, calculated killer, like the character in his thrillers. And then there's Spike."

"And what's his motive?"

"His is more of a mystery to me, but quite possibly the same as Dirk's. The only reason we know Spike also wrote a book early in his career is that Dirk told me. Spike labeled it an abysmal failure, which means it could have gotten a merciless review from our victim. I'm hesitant about Spike, though, because Dave's taken a liking to him. Heck, they're going fishing tomorrow or the next day, but if we can find out about his book, we'll know more."

One of Jake's most endearing qualities was his sense of humor, no matter how serious the situation. "In a good detective novel, we'd discover that Dirk planted that seed about Spike to send you down the wrong path. Classic misdirection. What do you think?"

"That I hate to suspect someone like Dirk whom I've grown to like. He's easy to talk to and has been encouraging about my writing. On the other hand, Dave also finds Spike easy to talk to. They have lots in common as journalists who focus on books and authors. And they're both ice cream lovers."

I was telling him about the Port Isaac ice cream parlor when Wendy texted me.

"Balvenie or Macallan's for Rhys. Brought Teacher's Blended Cream and left the half-full bottle with Spike Saturday night. Do I get an A+?"

When I showed Jake the text and his mouth dropped open, I knew Wendy had struck gold. "Teacher's. That's what I found at the cliff-side. Is Wendy shopping for scotch? What's this about?"

With my hands on my hips, I tapped my foot. "You might have mentioned that earlier. The only reason I've been looking into it is I heard they finished one bottle that night and started on a second one. And did Charlie tell you there were two whiskey tumblers on the back patio?"

He grimaced. "That's not a question I asked. I asked whether she served Teacher's, and she said no. Next, you'll tell me she dusted the tumblers for prints."

"Not quite, but tell me this. Did the bottle you found have a cap on it?"

"What do you think the answer is?"

"I think not. Because Charlie found a cap beneath the table where the glasses were. If the trash is still here, you could attempt to find it."

"A bottle cap instead of Cinderella's shoe. I think we can conclude it would fit without digging through the rubbish. Does this mean the three amigos moved the party to the patio? None of them mentioned leaving the front room."

He put two fingers to the bridge of his nose. "Where are you going with this, Leta? What are you not telling me?"

"The Teacher's came from Dirk. That's why he went to his

room Saturday night—to get more whiskey—and that's when Trevor Tarkington insulted him in the hallway. I can only think that he took the time to Google the guests, and he came prepared to be his usual charming self. Can you imagine? I don't know that he insulted every single one of us that night, but given another day, he probably would have."

"Okay. Dirk brought the second bottle of whiskey. That same bottle wound up on the cliff. It doesn't necessarily mean that Dirk was on that cliff with the victim, but it points that way."

"Except Dirk told Wendy he left it in the front room when he went to bed. Anyone could have picked it up." It was my turn to pinch the bridge of my nose. "Am I in danger of wanting it to be Spike because I've spent the least amount of time with him, and I don't know him well enough to like or dislike him?"

Jake shrugged. "The simple answer is yes. You don't like either Brax or Dirk for the crime because you like them as people. But likeable people can be as guilty as anyone else. When my constables find themselves questioning residents they've known forever, they have to guard against being biased one way or the other. Fortunately, or unfortunately, the more Cornwall police stations we close, the less often that's a problem. It's a double-edged sword—less bias but more area to cover with fewer stations."

"That's right. I'd forgotten you now work in Bodmin because they closed your station. When I thought earlier of driving to see you, I saw myself on the road to Truro."

As if choreographed, both of our phones buzzed with texts. Mine was from Dave, saying he was with Brax and asking where I was. Before I could respond, Jake leaped to his feet. "Crikey, I'm needed in Bude. What did I say about more area to cover?"

His phone rang before he could make it to the door. "DI Nancarrow. Yes, I'm on my way." As he opened the door, he glanced over his shoulder. "Leta, I'll ring you when I get a chance."

What now? I thought. I had my answer in Dave's next text. "Come next door ASAP. We've got answers."

CHAPTER SEVENTEEN

OUTSIDE, TWO CATS GREETED me. "Hagrid knows," meowed Christie.

"Knows what?"

"You asked who was on the patio drinking. Tell her, Hagrid."

The burly cat rubbed against my leg before sitting tall in front of me. "The man with the earring and the one with white hair."

It wasn't Dirk on the patio. "What else did you see, Hagrid?"

"They took a walk, and I followed them. They stumbled a lot, like Dave when Christie and I walked him here that night. She says she's never seen him like that before."

Oh my goodness. Did Hagrid witness the murder? I dropped to my haunches. "Hagrid, where did they go? Tell me everything you saw."

"They went straight to the clifftop and stood on the path facing the ocean for a long time. They drank, and I chased bugs. After a while, they followed me to the bench. By then, I'd found a mouse. Took them forever to get there, and they passed the bottle back and forth."

When Hagrid stopped to clean his paw, I wanted to shake him. "Please, can that wait? I need to hear what else you saw."

"That's about it. I left when the one with the earring tossed the bottle away and they started talking about dead soldiers. I took my mouse and went home to bed."

"And they were still sitting there when you left?"

Christie patted my knee with her paw. "That's what he said, Leta."

If cats could roll their eyes, that's probably what she would have done. "I know what he said, Christie. I just wanted to be sure."

The good news was that I now knew it was neither Brax nor Dirk on the clifftop with Trevor. There was only one man here who wore an earring. The bad news was the information had come from a cat. I imagined myself explaining to anyone beside Dickens that I had proof as to who was drinking with Trevor Saturday night.

I backtracked to get treats for my key witness and Christie. Hopefully, Brax and Dave had unearthed something similarly revealing that pointed to Spike.

Brax opened the door. "Leta, come on in. You're just in time to see the reactions Dad got from podcast listeners. It's like the saying about birds of a feather. Their comments about the books on the show were snarkier than Dad's. I think being polite has gone out of fashion."

"I don't doubt that. Claire gave us a handout of one- and two-star reviews received by award-winning authors. Only a few were constructive. The rest were unbelievably rude and hateful." I looked around. "Where's your mom?"

"She's napping. Spike interviewed her here for two hours, and she's worn out. And Dickens is with her, lying on the rug by the bed. He may have to go home with us."

Dave was sitting at the kitchen counter with a laptop and a scratchpad in front of him. "Don't worry, I already told him no way. Glad you're here. When you didn't respond right away, I was afraid you'd gone to Truro to find Jake. You won't believe what we found."

"And," Brax said, "we never would have found it if you hadn't known Dirk's real name. He and Dad exchanged several emails."

I wasn't sure I wanted to know. "About?"

"*Roses of Rebellion: The Courageous Story of a WWII French Resistance Fighter.* It's Dirk's book about his grandmother."

Dave turned the laptop around. "Here, Leta, look."

It was a split screen view of Trevor's review of the book next to an email. Dirk, or Patrick, had opened by agreeing the story sounded unbelievable, but that his grandmother's journal contained detailed accounts of the experience. What followed in that first email were screenshots of three journal pages. It was a harrowing tale of a nighttime mission in which two women died.

"Oh, my goodness. Her best friend died as she watched. Do you have your father's reply? Was he convinced after seeing this?"

Dave scrolled to Trevor's response. "Much as you want to believe your grandmother was a heroine, her journal is the stuff of fantasy. No real resistance fighter would have risked putting this on paper for fear it would be discovered. When you say this book is based on a true story, you are misleading your readers."

I looked up. "Harsh, but not as bad as I expected."

"There's more."

As Dave continued to scroll, I saw that Patrick had tried to convince Trevor of the truth of the story by forwarding notes from interviews he'd done with his grandmother's surviving compatriots. He also attached a photo of a faded rose pressed between the pages of what appeared to be a French recipe book.

Trevor's response was brutal: "Face it, either she's delusional or she lied to you."

I gasped. "How could he be so sure, and even if he was, why

was he so cruel? Why not let it go?"

Brax winced. "I have no idea, other than that my father was pigheaded in all manner of ways. Did he fancy himself an expert on the French Resistance? I doubt it. Did he think, as he said in his review, that the story was histrionic, overblown, and whatnot? Probably, but that doesn't change the nastiness of his replies. I think we can all agree that calling Dirk's grandmother a liar was beyond the pale."

Pointing to the screen, Dave scrolled one more time. "Look at Dirk's response, sent months later."

"*May you roast in hell. Thankfully, my grandmother never saw our correspondence. Your vitriolic review was hard enough for her to bear. I won't bother to share the condolence letters we received last month when word of her death reached her small village in France. Unlike you, others recognized the truth in her story. A handful even shared memories of Gran's bravery passed down from their grandparents. Her story lives on.*"

Looking from Dave to Brax and back to the screen, I was speechless. Would I have been that polite in Dirk's shoes?

Finally, Dave said what I was thinking. "Can you believe how civil he was? How calm?"

Brax agreed. "I honestly can't believe he didn't tell Dad where to go. Roast in hell was mild."

Spike was on the cliff, but Dirk had a motive. Did a strong motive trump opportunity? "Does this make Dirk our leading suspect?"

"I think so, Tuppence. Don't you?"

How do I tell them Spike was on the cliff? "I know I put him on the list, but his emails seem pretty mild." I squinted at the dates. "And they date back to 2001. But if none of the other names showed up, I guess his name moves to the top."

Brax shrugged. "We looked for all of them, even Charlie and

George and Duncan because readers occasionally wrote Dad, too, usually about his Dallas Steele books. But only Dirk or Patrick showed up. Heck, we even sorted by first names to see if any of the other authors might have used a different surname."

"Goodness, when you said you were organized, you weren't kidding."

"I believe I said boringly organized," he quipped.

I thought aloud. "We still have a handful of people without alibis. But Dirk is the only one we can find who had a past, so to speak, with your dad—and a reason to bear him a grudge. The big question mark for me is Spike's book. Dave, did you find out anything more about it?"

"Nope. I asked when I caught up with him right after lunch. All he would say was it's not a chapter in his life he wants to revisit."

"But how does a book simply disappear with no record?"

Brax chimed in. "It could be a combination of things. He could have self-published it or used a vanity press and then withdrawn it from publication. As closemouthed as he is about the darned thing, I suspect it doesn't reflect well on him."

"Doesn't that seem odd to you guys?"

Dave shrugged his shoulders. "Yes, but if it was horribly amateur, he may see it as a blot on his record. That's all I can think of."

I think he has something more to hide than an embarrassing book, as in a connection to Trevor Tarkington. But how am I going to get proof of that? Hagrid's testimony is hardly going to do the job.

CHAPTER EIGHTEEN

As we returned to our cottage, Dave suggested we visit Port Isaac. "It's the kind of town you love, and I hate for you to miss it. Not to mention, I consider it my duty to introduce you to the ice cream shop."

"That would be a welcome distraction, and I can tell you on the way what Jake had to say. Except I have to tell you the most important development now. You're in the clear."

He grinned at the idea of being cleared by a romance writer and two cats. "You know, I was never worried about being a suspect. I knew Jake would figure it out eventually."

Following us inside, Christie made her wishes known. "Take me. I haven't been anywhere in days."

Dave scratched her head. "Do you want food, princess?"

She got her point across by darting to her backpack. She pawed it and meowed, "No. I want to go with you."

"You're a funny little thing. If I didn't know better, I'd think you knew we were taking a ride." He opened the top of the backpack, and she crawled in and turned around with her head sticking out. "Leta, I think she wants to go."

Dave pulled into the car park up top. "Spike and I made the

mistake of trying to drive in town the other day. What a night-mare." He unbuckled the backpack and put it on his shoulders. When he moved to Astonbury, Christie made it known that she preferred his back to mine, and that had been our routine ever since.

She stuck her pink nose in the air. "I smell salt air. Hurry."

Reaching over his shoulder, Dave scratched her nose. "Does that meow mean you're ready for us to get a move on?"

"Isn't that what I just said?"

I pulled out the list I'd printed before we left home. "They have lots of shops for such a small village. How many did you visit with Spike?" When he faked a groan, I nudged him. "We don't have to see them all today. For instance, we can skip the hardware store."

"Hey, you don't know what you're missing. But I'm game, as long as we don't pop into every single one. I didn't make it to the bookshop the other day, and I feel obliged to check the pastry shop and the ice cream parlor again."

"Of course you do. For now, let's stroll to the harbor. On the climb back up, we'll both deserve a treat."

Glimpses of the harbor came and went as we walked down the narrow, twisty lane and peered into the shop windows. At the bottom, the view of the sparkling water with the cliffs stretching along either side was breathtaking.

Dave pointed to the right. "Those cliffs are called The Rumps, and that's where the Clifftop Retreat is located. From here, you can see the beach where Spike and I plan to fish, weather permit-ting."

"This would have been the perfect place for a destination wedding, with plenty for our guests to do in town. Too bad a body on the beach has ruined that idea." As we turned to start the uphill climb, we named other picturesque villages to visit as potential wedding spots before we returned home.

We retraced our steps and stopped in the bookshop tucked away on a side street. It made sense that the Wycliffe mysteries were prominently displayed in the mystery section, as the series took place in Cornwall. I'd enjoyed the TV series but had never picked up the books. I grabbed *Wycliffe and the Three-Toed Pussy*, the first book. Reading the placard about the author, I discovered he'd lived in Fowey, the town our writing group had visited.

When I found Dave, he was in the travel section. "I'm expanding on your idea of a destination wedding. Why not France or Greece? Since Ellie offered us her villa in Provence for our honeymoon, we could look for an interesting wedding venue nearby. Or we could get married on a Greek island and honeymoon there. What do you think?"

"That's a grand idea, and we'll have to visit both places in person before we can make an informed decision. Wouldn't you agree?"

With two travel books and one mystery, we climbed to the ice cream shop. Dave chose a two-scoop cone of Double Chocolate, and I ordered a cup of Vanilla Lavender, a flavor I'd enjoyed on my last trip to Cornwall. Sitting at an inside table was a necessity as the wind was picking up.

"Now, tell me about Jake," Dave said between licks. "I take it he's still focused on Brax as his chief suspect, or you would have already told me differently."

I explained Jake's belief that money was as good a motive as hate or loathing, and he saw Brax as having both. Dave nodded in agreement with everything I said until I reached the techno alibi part.

"Seriously? There must be apps for everything under the sun, but I can't see your average Joe knowing about them. When are you going to tell Jake about Dirk? That should take the heat off Brax."

My hesitation gave me away.

"You don't want it to be Brax or Dirk, do you?" he asked.

I admitted as much. "But if you take them out of the picture, that only leaves Spike, Oliver, Charlie, and George without alibis. Who would you put at the top of that list?"

"Not Charlie or George. I'd choose a writer or a journalist, meaning Oliver or Spike. Oliver's so mild-mannered, I can't see him pushing someone off a cliff, though you never know. And, much the way you feel about Dirk, I don't want to think it's Spike. He's just so darned affable. Of course, we haven't seen a display of temper from either of them—but again, it doesn't mean it's not there beneath a calm facade."

"It occurs to me that this business of sleuthing makes it difficult to take people at face value. When I worked in Human Resources, I thought I was a decent judge of character, but now I routinely second-guess myself."

A crease formed between Dave's brows. "I think you're right. I used to believe my first impressions were always spot-on, but I've learned they're not. Except for you. I was right about you!"

I beamed before shifting gears. "Tell me more about Spike. What did you two talk about other than fishing and ice cream?"

"Well, those are clearly the most important topics. Let me grab a cookie, and I'll think about it. Want one?"

While he ate his second dessert, I offered Christie my ice cream cup. She was finicky about her wet food but had no problem licking the cup I put beneath her nose. "Does that meet with your approval, little girl?"

"Yes. Why don't we have this stuff at home?" Ignoring her question, I prompted Dave to answer my question.

"I can't believe I didn't tell you his kayaking recommendation.

I was looking at a company in Padstow, but Spike thinks Cornish Coast Adventures in Port Quin is a better option, especially if we want to explore the sea caves."

"How does that work? Do you beach the kayak and walk into the caves?"

"Yup. If you can't bear the thought of going in, you can stay with the kayaks. Or you can stick your head in the entrance and get a good look that way." That made the idea seem more palatable to me.

"Other than fishing and kayaking, we talked about our backgrounds as two journalists who started as crime reporters. We couldn't believe we both chose journalism as our major and stuck to it. I mentioned my high school reunion and how so few of my classmates had careers anything like what they'd envisioned, other than the obvious ones like doctor or lawyer."

"I wonder how often that's the case, like me only briefly teaching high school English. What did he have to say about his classmates?"

"He's only kept in touch with one or two, and he avoids reunions." Dave hesitated. "It's a heartbreaking story, Leta. His twin sister died when they were in college. It's over twenty years ago, but you can tell when he talks about her that the loss still haunts him."

I shuddered. "That's awful. Losing a sibling would be hard enough, but a twin and so young? I can't imagine."

"I know. I kept picturing my sister the whole time he talked about it. Sienna, that's her name, died in a horrendous car wreck their junior year.

"Leta, I felt like all my words were inadequate. What do you say to something like that? After I said I was sorry several different ways, he said he'd learn to dwell on the happy times—her sense of humor, watching her at gymnastics, and just hanging out."

We went on in that vein until we both ran out of words. "Enough of that," Dave said. "On a different note, did I mention this isn't the first time Spike's interviewed Issa?"

"No. That's interesting."

"He really admires her, and he's read all her books. Have you read *Memories of Spring*? That's his favorite. Apparently, they've been corresponding for years."

"It's funny. I know you enjoyed *Summer Solstice*, but I can't imagine many men read her books. As we know, even her husband didn't read them all."

He raised a brow. "I can only imagine how I'd feel if you hadn't read my book. That would be hard to take."

"Trust me. If you don't read mine, I'll never forgive you. Especially since it was your idea."

"Since I expect to show up in one or two of the adventures, I'll have no choice but to read them."

I handed him the backpack. "Let's get one more glimpse of the harbor and head back to the inn. If we leave now, we'll make it to happy hour."

Walking toward our cottage, I was surprised to see Dickens bounding toward me. "Leta, we went for a walk."

Behind him came Brax and Issa. I was happy to see her walking with her cane tucked beneath her arm and recalled Brax saying she had good days and bad ones.

She called out as they got closer. "I see you've been shopping for books instead of writing one. What treasure did you find?"

"Let's call it research, since it's an Inspector Wycliffe mystery.

Have you read any of them?"

"Can't say that I have. I've got Ann Patchett's latest on my bedside table. She's one of my favorite authors."

I showed them our purchases and explained about destination wedding research. When Dave came up behind me, a surprised smile appeared on Issa's face. "A cat in a backpack?" She looked at Brax. "Like that cat who rides in a bicycle basket in that book you gave me."

Dave tilted toward Issa so she could pet Christie. "We haven't taken her on a bicycle ride yet. That may be a bridge too far for the princess."

Christie's response was no surprise. "I don't know about bridges, but there's no way you're getting me on a bike."

As Dave and Issa discussed their fondness for following Nala the cat's adventures on Instagram, Brax pulled me aside. "Mom's mood is so improved; I didn't want to bring up anything about Dad in front of her. I found his book, or at least a version with a later date than what his editor had. Speaking with the housekeeper reminded me I hadn't checked Dad's special email account, the one he used only for his editor. I'm so accustomed to seeing it as off-limits, it didn't occur to me. Stupid, I know."

"I'm not following you, Brax."

"What I found was an email in his draft folder, an email with a manuscript dated August 2nd. I immediately forwarded it to his editor, explaining where I found it. Unfortunately, I can tell from reading their back-and-forth that it's not what he's looking for."

"What do you mean?"

"They'd been arguing about the last chapter for months, and this last email looks like Dad's final word on the subject. I think he was stringing his editor along and never intended to change a thing. When I compared this latest version to the previous one, I could tell that the ending hadn't changed. All he did was change the date, which could explain why he didn't bother to back it up to the cloud."

"What was the point of contention?"

His face flushed. "That was crystal clear. He killed off Dallas Steele, his main character. He said it was time, and he referenced Colin Dexter's Morse dying in the last book. The Dallas Steele series had to be a cash cow for the publisher, so it's no wonder they were trying to change his mind."

My mouth dropped open. "You don't lightly kill off your main character. What could have prompted that?"

"He didn't tell me what he was planning, but I'd like to believe he wanted to focus on Mom. If you've read anything about him, you know he gave up his editing career to be at home with my sister when she was diagnosed with leukemia. I suspect he'd finally gotten to the point where he could no longer ignore Mom's Parkinson's. He may have been argumentative and overbearing, but he loved my mother. When he was berating her that first night, he mentioned their waning years, and how her writing another book wasn't how he envisioned them."

"Oh Brax, I can only imagine how she'll feel when she hears all this. It makes his death all the more heartbreaking."

As soon as I walked into our cottage, I shared Brax's discovery with Dave. "He sees it as a sign that Trevor had accepted Issa's condition and wanted to be by her side. Brax didn't use these words, but I think he also saw it as a testament to his love for her. How ineffably sad."

Dave must have sensed my mood, because he suggested we

skip happy hour. I readily agreed. When I returned to the sitting room, after an abbreviated fluff and dust and quick change of clothes, he handed me a glass of wine. "What do you say we have our own happy hour here, and time our arrival for the last fifteen minutes of the cocktail party?"

"I couldn't agree more. I was already small-talked out, what with the story about Spike's sister and reading what Dirk wrote to Trevor Tarkington. Add what Brax just told me, and it will be all I can do to say 'pass the salt' at dinner."

"I'm sure the concern about Trevor's book was never on Jake's radar, but do you plan to contact him about Dirk? Or are you considering speaking with Dirk first—to see what he has to say? With me by your side, of course."

"It crossed my mind to tell him what we know and suggest he tell Jake himself. I've done that before." It was with Toby and Peter in our small village—two men who would have been seen as suspects if they hadn't gone to Gemma to confess their connection to a murder victim. She didn't rush to judgment and take either of them away in handcuffs. Instead, she listened and used the information to help solve the crime. With a bit of help from me, that is.

"I like that idea. We're neither of us convinced he's the murderer, and it's not as though we're worried he's on a killing spree. It's like Brax. He has means, motive, and opportunity, but we believe in his alibi. Unfortunately, as far as we know, Dirk doesn't have one. Too bad a romance author didn't see him being escorted to bed by two cats."

I had to keep telling myself that we were in no danger from Spike either, and that being on the cliff that night wasn't proof he pushed Trevor to his death. But it was certainly more proof than that offered by a decades-old string of emails. Why would an ancient grudge flare up into murder? Could the hate mail have led us away from the true motive? Was the spark that lit the flame something recent?

CHAPTER NINETEEN

WENDY MOTIONED DAVE AND me over to where she and Dirk were chatting. "Dirk just told me he's in talks with Claire about a new book. Of course, I suggested he speak with you, Dave, about how you adore working with her."

Dave slapped Dirk on the back. "You can't go wrong with Claire. She's an amazing editor, and her fiancé, Simon, is equally gifted as the PR Director. I take it you're going in a new direction, since Harris House doesn't publish thrillers."

As they did a deep dive into Dirk's idea, Wendy pulled me aside. "So, what's up? Did you see Jake today?"

I gave her the bullet points—Brax still a suspect, Dave in the clear, the bottle of Teacher's, Dirk's connection to Trevor Tarkington—everything except Hagrid's account of who was on the cliff with Trevor the night of the murder. Wendy might be my best friend, but even she didn't know I could talk to the animals.

Her eyes widened. "You mean I've just spent the day quizzing the chief suspect?" She darted a look at Dirk and Dave. "How could he be so nonchalant with his answers? He doesn't act guilty at all."

Whispering, I turned her toward the windows. "I wonder the

same thing. When he told you it was a bottle of Teacher's he shared, wouldn't it have reminded him he'd left it at the cliff? That he hadn't seen it since he . . . pushed a man to his death? Could he be so cold-blooded that he wouldn't bat an eye? Let's just say I have my doubts."

We both jumped when a man spoke behind us. "Who's cold-blooded? The killer in your Constable James book?"

It was Spike, and I crossed my fingers he didn't realize we weren't talking about a fictional murder. "Yes. I'm considering a woman as the villain. As a former crime reporter, do you think a woman could be a cold-blooded killer?"

He blithely launched into the statistics about male versus female serial killers and the numbers of one-off murders committed by women versus men. "If it's a crime of passion, it could easily be a woman."

I could say the same thing about him as Wendy had about Dirk. Knowing what I did, I marveled at his nonchalance.

"Have you run that by Issa? Why don't you join the two of us for dinner, Leta? We plan to discuss how the coaching sessions are going, but I'm sure we could spare a few minutes for brainstorming."

"That would be perfect. I could use fresh thoughts about the plot."

After George took our orders, Issa asked about Port Isaac. "I understand from Spike that the streets are steep. I had my heart set on visiting, but I'm not sure now."

"I imagine if you and Brax go early in the morning, there would be less traffic, and he could drive to the harbor. You might be able to visit a few shops that way, too."

Spike agreed with that idea and explained to Issa why he'd invited me to join them. "So, Leta, let's hear more about the idea for your villain."

"Issa, you're aware that both mine and Wendy's books are based on real cases from our village. It's helpful that we know the local constable and detective inspector so well, and that they're free with the particulars." *No harm in a white lie now and then*, I thought.

"For the book Wendy's working on now, the victim died from strangulation, and the killer was a woman who flew into a rage. No one suspected her because she came across as caring and calm, until she didn't. They were focused on the victim's estranged spouse."

Spike interjected. "Because it's so often the family, right? But not in that case."

"Yes, the arresting officer described her as delusional, and I experienced that trait myself. If she hadn't lost it in front of me, they might never have realized it was her, instead of the wife."

Issa squinted. "That sounds intriguing. She killed him in a rage. Did the police ever establish what triggered it?"

Dare I say this in front of Spike? In for a penny, in for a pound. "We . . . they surmised it was something the victim said or did in the moment, but of course, she didn't say. My problem is how to make it believable. It happened in real life, but the readers won't know that. I need to make up a convincing motive. What does it take for someone to snap like that? Did the victim say or do something that set her off? Or did she already have it in her head to kill him when she approached him?" Another white lie. I knew exactly what happened.

Spike touched Issa's arm. "May I?"

At her nod, he proceeded. "It's been a while, but when I first left the crime beat, I wrote an opinion piece on gang crimes. The authorities put the violence down to gang mentality, but what is that? Is it a hair-trigger temper in the heat of the moment or a smoldering hatred that leads to pre-meditated murder? If your local DI doesn't know for sure, you could choose one or the other and flesh it out."

Issa sipped her wine. "I can hear a tattooed teen on *Law & Order* saying, 'He dissed me.' And then the gun comes out. The diss, as they call it, could be a look or a word. That's all it takes."

Does Spike know I suspect him? Is he toying with me? "I like the heat of the moment idea. The motive could be love. She's the mistress, madly in love with him, and he utters a stinging insult or tells her it's over."

Thank goodness George delivered our salads, and we shifted to the topic of Issa's coaching sessions and how the authors had a variety of challenges. I was off the hook for the rest of the meal.

When I declined dessert and went to tell Dave I'd see him at our cottage, Wendy headed me off. "Mum and I are calling it a night. I have an idea for the next chapter in *The Incident at the Inn* and want to write for a bit."

Dave called me over to Brax's table. "Leta, we're thinking of a trip to the pub in Port Isaac. Dirk says The Golden Lion boasts a selection from several local breweries. Do you want to join us?"

The look on my face was answer enough. "What did I tell you guys? There's no way Leta's going with us, and Wendy's already declined. Shall we make a general announcement and be done with it?"

Dirk clapped his hands to get everyone's attention. "Since we have tonight off, we're putting together a group to visit the local pub. Any takers?"

When Spike was the only one to accept the invitation, I pointed to Brax. "Given the track record of the three amigos, can I count on you to be the adult in the room?"

They all got a good laugh out of that, and Dave swore that nothing but beer would pass his lips. Brax offered to drive before whispering in my ear. "I'll trade you, Leta. I'll look out for Dave if you'll do the same for Mom. Belle's moving back to her room with Wendy, and I'll feel better about taking this break if I know you'll look in on her. I plan to stay in Dad's room when I get back."

That settled, I sat with Issa and joked about boys being boys as the group dispersed. With Dave gone, it would have been a perfect night to write, but I knew that wasn't going to happen. I had too much on my mind.

Oliver, Evie, and Nora grabbed blankets and moved to the back patio, and Claire joined Issa and me by the fire in the front room. When she suggested an after-dinner drink, we settled on Kahlua.

"Are you two joining us tomorrow for the visit to Tintagel?" Claire asked. "It's a shorter trip than the one to Fowey and a must-see for King Arthur fans. The original plan was to go in the morning, but with rain in the forecast until midday, we may shift to after lunch. We can switch the Point of View Palooza and writing time to the morning."

Issa tilted her head. "I'd love to see Tintagel, and I brought my motorized wheelchair in case I felt up to it. I never could have made it to the island before they installed the new bridge."

"It is so worth the trip, Issa. Wendy and I did it last year. You won't be able to see every bit of the outcroppings and the excavation sites in a wheelchair, but you'll get a feel for it. You may be able to use your cane in a few spots, and we can help you."

She agreed to give it a try just as her phone vibrated with a text. "What wonderful news. Karen just called Brax. She must have finally come out of the woods, and she's calling DI Nancarrow now."

I explained to Claire that Karen was Brax's girlfriend and told them both about the call duration app, which dumbfounded them as it had me. "Honestly, when Jake described it, I thought he was making it up. I'm glad it's off the table now."

When Issa excused herself to visit the ladies' room, it was a good opportunity for me to ask Claire about Dirk. "I'm going to be nosey. Do you think you'll take Dirk on as a client?"

"It's quite likely. He's a good strong writer, and his thrillers are popular. You know how we at Harris House like World War II fiction and non-fiction alike, so he could be a good fit if he pursues the French Resistance angle. He's going to get me a copy of *Roses of Rebellion*, and we'll go from there."

"Did he mention that Trevor Tarkington was highly critical of it?"

"Yes. But I know better than to let that cloud my judgment. I agreed with a handful of Trevor's reviews, though I would never have been as harsh as he was. I'll form my own opinion."

"Claire, how much do you know about Spike? I've been told he wrote a book, but I can't find it when I Google him."

"That doesn't surprise me. It's not every journalist who can make a successful shift to writing fiction, and from what I've heard, he's not proud of his attempt."

I asked why it didn't at least show up online, even if it was out of print. "I easily found Dirk's earlier book, and it's under a different name."

"That's because his Patrick Owens author bio includes a reference to Dirk Blackthorne being a pen name. Just like Nora Roberts makes no secret of also writing as J. D. Robb. But in Spike's case, I imagine he wouldn't want his slick journalist's name associated with his real name. Remember he mentioned being asked to change it for the crime beat."

"Wait. What was it? Was it Simon or Stanley?"

"No. Seymour."

"So, if I Google Seymour O'Malley, I might find his book."

She chuckled. "Oh no. That won't do it. Try Seymour Jones.

That's his real name. I only know because when we reimburse his expenses, that's the name on the account. You can see why he changed it to sound like a tough as nails crime reporter. There's no reference to his fiction attempt in his bio. Too bad he didn't try writing a crime novel. Spike O'Malley would make a great name for a crime fiction author, wouldn't it?"

I had another question on the tip of my tongue, but Issa called my name. "Leta, I hate to ask you, but would you walk with me back to my cottage, please? I feel sure I can make it without help, but Brax would never let me hear the end of it if he found out I went on my own."

"Not a problem, Issa. I'm not a night owl by any means. Claire, will it be a 9 a.m. start tomorrow?"

"Yes, and I'll allow time to grab jackets and walking shoes if the Tintagel trip turns out to be after breakfast. Otherwise, we'll meet in the library."

At the door to her cottage, Issa invited me in for tea. "I always brew a pot of chamomile tea close to bedtime. Would you care for a cup?"

Sensing she wasn't ready to be alone with her thoughts, I accepted. Something to calm the swirling of my brain couldn't hurt. "Point me in the right direction, Issa, and I'll make it. Do you want to change into your nightclothes while I'm here? I'll put some logs on the fire, too."

I had the fire blazing and the tea ready when she returned in her robe. With Issa settled in the chair closest to the fireplace, I sank onto the couch with my tea. "Oh, lavender! There's lavender in this tea. Where did you find this?"

"We picked it up at the Farm Shop in Boscastle on the drive here. I'll have to get Brax to stop back by so I can stock up."

After a second sip, I leaned my head back. Was it only this morning I'd read the disturbing opening line in Issa's book? It felt like ages ago. And from that moment on, data had come at me from all directions—Jake, Hagrid, Dave, Brax, and Wendy. The issue was sorting the relevant from the irrelevant and connecting the dots. *Seymour Jones!* I nearly spilled my tea when I sat straight up. Issa might know.

"What is it, Leta?"

"A random thought. Did you know Spike wrote a book?"

"Dear Spike. Yes, long before we became regular pen pals."

At my feigned look of surprise, she elaborated. "The first time I heard from him was when he read *Memories of Spring*. The plight of the daughter resonated with him, so much so that he quoted passages in his email to me."

"I must admit I haven't read that one, Issa. The story of the widow in *Summer Solstice* tugged at my heartstrings because her emotions were so like mine. Was that what happened with Spike and the daughter?"

"Yes. Tess in the book survives a suicide attempt. Her regrets and her struggles touched him. It was Spike's mother who suggested he read the book because her daughter, his twin, committed suicide."

Suicide? Why did he tell Dave it was a car accident? "He told Dave his sister died when they were juniors at college, but Dave must have misunderstood. He thought it was in a car crash."

Issa pursed her lips. "No. Her boyfriend died, and she nearly did. As it was, she sustained horrific injuries to her legs and underwent multiple surgeries. Spike wanted to defer his senior year and stay home with her, but she was adamant that he go back.

"That's the saddest part. Not long after he returned to school, she committed suicide. His mother found her the morning of yet another surgery, an empty vial of pain pills on the nightstand and a note clutched in her hand. Essentially, she said she couldn't face the prospect of never regaining the full use of her legs."

"How horrible for all of them. His poor mom, and how must Spike have felt? Am I right that his sister was a gymnast?"

"Yes, and quite a good one, according to Spike."

"And he saw his sister in the story of Tess in your book."

"Yes. He alluded to it being an inspiration, but it wasn't until he surprised me with a copy of his book two years later that I realized what he meant. It inspired him to write a novel about losing a sister. Thank goodness, he included a handwritten note explaining who he was. I never would have connected the name Seymour Jones with the Spike O'Malley who'd written me about *Memories of Spring*."

She frowned. "I'm not saying anything I haven't said to Spike, or he hasn't said to himself. It was an ill-conceived effort from the start. He's an accomplished journalist whose writing stands out for its brevity and clarity. Think of Dragnet and 'just the facts.'

"He had no idea how to write a moving narrative. Simply put, he overcompensated with flowery language. A good critique group could have helped him see that, but he wrote the book in isolation. I have an image of him pounding it out on an old Royal typewriter, though I know it was a laptop. And then he self-published it. At a bare minimum, he should have sent it to an editor."

"How did you respond to him, Issa? I can't imagine you were harsh given the personal nature of the book."

"Because I was in the throes of completing my next book, I dropped him a quick line to that effect, saying I would set aside time to read it. A month passed, and he beat me to the punch with an email containing the handful of reviews he'd gotten. They were overwhelmingly negative, describing his writing as cloying and mawkish. But the worst of them was Trevor's. How on earth he stumbled across *Losing Sarah* was a mystery to me until I reread the blurb. I knew it was the mention of suicide."

"I don't understand."

She drew in a deep breath before asking if I knew that their daughter died of leukemia. When I nodded, she told me that Trevor had gone on to work tirelessly as a fundraiser for St. Jude's. "Not long after Elizabeth died, a friend's fourteen-year-old daughter committed suicide. Trevor reacted with a strange mixture of sadness and outrage, and outrage won out. That a young girl who had a full life ahead of her chose death was more than he could bear. You may recall he mentioned *The Virgin Suicides* the other night?"

"Yes. He said he reviewed it."

"Right or wrong, rational or not, he made it his mission to skewer books or programs that dared to imply that suicide was in any way acceptable. You or I might have read the same book and not sensed any hint of that, but not Trevor. *Revolutionary Road*, *Thirteen Reasons Why*, even Kate Chopin's *The Awakening* all fell victim to his perverse outrage. Conversely, he praised books and documentaries about Christopher Reeve, Michael J. Fox and others who didn't give up in the face of adversity. Trevor was a complicated man."

"And Spike's book fell victim to his outrage, as you put it?"

"Yes, and that's when I finally read it. I sent Spike a lengthy email about it being a tragic story that deserved better and offered to speak with him about how to rework it. Trust me, the timing was terrible for me, with a book tour coming up, but somehow, I felt it was the least I could do."

Their phone conversations and ongoing correspondence had evolved into a deep friendship. "We were like old-time pen pals and still are. We didn't meet in person until he came to New York to interview another author. It's funny, isn't it, how you can have conversations with friends that you'd never have with your child or partner? My sister and Spike were those people for me. And now, it's only Spike. He's been incredibly attentive this week, listening as I talk through my jumbled emotions. I'm still doing that, but now I'm also reflecting on my writing journey for his story. And Trevor is so much a part of that journey. As you said, it's good to remember the happy times."

I was glad she'd absorbed what I'd said to her earlier about good memories. "Yes, that's what got me through the shock of Henry's death. Funerals and memorial services are more for the living, I think, so that we can remind ourselves of the happiness we experienced. Laughing about the good times leads to tears, but it's worth it."

After pouring more tea for Issa, I straightened the kitchen and took Dickens for a short walk. Christie and Hagrid fell in behind us as we walked toward the cliff.

Hearing why Trevor felt so strongly about suicide revealed another side of him. It didn't excuse his confrontational behavior, but it explained some of it. What would it be like to live with a man whose every response was venomous? Was the aggression a way to mask his profound unhappiness?

I turned right on the cliff path and followed the lights to the bench. "Enough, Dickens, this is the point where Belle would chide me for dabbling in psychology." Pulling my phone from my parka, I googled *Losing Sarah*, and there it was, listed on Amazon. The brief author page told me that Seymour Jones lived in London and that the inspiration for this debut novel was his sister Sienna. It made no mention that Seymour Jones was a journalist.

Hitting the back arrow, I read the blurb and saw that only used copies of the book were available. Brax had been right in suggesting that Spike could have pulled it from publication. I scrolled through the reviews. They were a mixed bag, but the theme was consistent. The overly emotional writing detracted from what was a tragic story. One review said the author had overdone the adjectives. Perhaps that was the problem. In trying to shake off his crisp journalistic style, Spike had gone to the opposite extreme.

There, on the second page of reviews, was Trevor's. It was pure Snarkington, and he lambasted the weak main character as much as he did the amateur writing. One side of my brain said, "Okay, you know why he feels this way," while the other side asked, "How could he write this?"

The question of whether Spike wrote to Trevor was irrelevant. He had good reason to despise him. Either that or Spike was a much better person than I was. It didn't matter whether the criticism was warranted. It had been worded to wound.

Texting Dave the link to the book, I told him to read the Snarkington review. A fine sprinkle had started again, and I wondered whether it would become the full-fledged storm Claire had mentioned.

Hagrid had disappeared, but Christie leaped into my lap. "Is there room for me inside your jacket?"

Dickens, of course, was reveling in the damp weather. "Let's go, Dickens. Christie and I are ready to sit in front of the fire." He grumbled a tad and led the way to Issa's cottage as though he knew she needed him. Letting him in, I called goodnight.

As I shooed Christie into our cottage, Dave's return text arrived. "Good job. Are you in bed yet?"

His response to "almost" was to suggest I not wait up and to let me know that fishing in the morning was out. I brought in more wood and added logs to the stove before changing into my gown. With my new Wycliffe mystery, I stretched out on the couch. I saw the cast of the television show in my head as I read. When my phone rang with its Billy Joel ringtone, I knew it was Dave. He'd loaded "Until the Night" on my phone a month ago as a surprise. "Leta, you haven't turned out the light yet, have you?"

"No. Reading my new book."

"Spike is standing beside me, and you should see the look on his face. He's horrified that you found his 'poor excuse for a novel,' as he puts it. Hold on." I heard talking in the background, something about forgetting I'd ever seen it. "Yes, I'll tell her. He wants you to promise you won't tell a soul. Says it will ruin his reputation as a hard-hitting journalist if anyone makes the connection."

Laughter erupted in the background. "Of course, I already told Dirk and Brax, but he's swearing them to silence and offering bribes of beer. I told him he'd have to up his game for you and flowers might do the trick."

After more back-and-forth from the peanut gallery, he signed off. My thoughts were a jumble. How must Spike feel as they joked about his book, none of them knowing its personal nature? Had Dave taken the time to read Seymour Jones's author bio? Had he read the review from Trevor? Was I putting too much faith in Hagrid's eyewitness statement?

I felt more and more sure that Spike had pushed Trevor off the cliff. Whether it was planned prior to the workshop or from the moment Trevor made his callous comment about suicide was immaterial. Because both men were drinking, it might even have been an accident triggered by yet another comment. The why and how didn't matter.

What mattered was that he had the strongest motive, combined with means and opportunity. If my conclusion was wrong, no harm done. But if I was right, Dave needed to be careful.

Spike knew of our sleuthing exploits. Given what he'd seen on the walls of our cottage, he'd have every reason to be concerned now that we knew about his book—every reason to think we might be on to him.

I couldn't help myself. I called Dave to warn him, but it rolled to voicemail. I texted. "Call me ASAP." As the minutes crawled by, I replayed Issa's words in my head. Sienna, Spike's sister, committed suicide. Trevor described the character Sarah as weak. If the two men corresponded, I had no doubt that Trevor's response would have been over the top horrific.

Until I could ask Brax to check, there was no way to know for sure. Perhaps Spike never wrote Trevor, but what if he did? Of the motives on the wall, it was loathing that leaped out. Spike had to loathe Trevor even before the panel discussion.

Again, I called Dave. This time when it rolled to voicemail, I did my best to explain that he needed to be wary and why. I used the words, "Don't be alone with Spike," and asked him to call me back. As long as he stuck with Brax and Dirk, he'd be safe. Short of getting in the car and driving to the pub, I didn't know what else to do.

I shifted the black furball from my lap and stuck my feet in my slippers. "Enough! We'll figure out next steps in the morning."

Christie did a down doggie stretch and followed me to the bedroom. With visions of Dave and me talking everything through over steaming mugs of coffee, I drifted off to sleep.

CHAPTER TWENTY

I BREATHED A SIGH of relief when I felt Dave snuggle against my back and wrap his arm around my waist. Sometime later, dreaming about fresh coffee and toast, I rolled over and reached for him, but he wasn't there. I opened one eye and saw light coming from the kitchen. *Is he really making toast?*

Why on earth is he up at this hour? Pulling on my robe, I padded to the kitchen, where I found a still-warm, half-empty mug of coffee. Next to it lay Dave's phone and a note. "Gone fishing. Break in the rain."

Staring in disbelief at the words, I registered that he was alone with Spike at the same time as I heard a thud against the door and Christie screeching, "Leta, come quick." When I threw open the door, she sprang into my arms. "He won't listen. Hurry."

As she took off toward the cliff, I chased after her. "Where is he, Christie? Is he on the beach?" Up ahead, the motion detector lights came on as she darted past them to the right. They lit up all down the path as she ran.

When I turned onto the path, I saw a beam of light in the brush and someone shadowboxing in the glow of the path lights. At least, that's what it looked like.

"Dave, is that you?" When he turned toward me, he was attempting to pry one cat from his chest as another one climbed his legs.

"Leta, help me! They've gone mad."

"Christie, Hagrid, what are you doing?" It was all I could do to unlatch Hagrid's claws from Dave's chest. "Christie, get down."

Panting, Dave bent over with his hands on his knees, while Hagrid meowed, "Stay put!"

A faint voice came from the beach. "Dave, are you coming?"

Leaving Dave to catch his breath, I grabbed the flashlight from the brush and followed the cats. They halted at the top of the rock path and took up positions side by side. For Dave to meet Spike on the beach, he'd have to take the steep rock path down the cliff.

"Look," Christie meowed.

Near the waterline, I saw what looked like a fishing rod sticking up from the sand. I didn't know what I was supposed to make of that until Christie meowed again. "Look behind me."

I squatted and shined the flashlight just beyond the cats as Christie turned and pawed at a silver thread. Leaning forward, I peered at the first stone step. "It's . . . it's fishing line."

Dave came up behind me. "Leta, what are you doing?"

With my free hand, I pointed to the line stretched taut across the path. "Keeping you from killing yourself. Look."

When he squatted beside me, Christie put her paws on his knee and hissed. "Back up."

I pointed the flashlight at the foot of the steps where it hit the beach. The beam wasn't strong, but I could make out the figure of a man. It had to be Spike.

Dave pulled me to my feet and grabbed the flashlight. "Spike, what the hell?"

No response, only the sound of the ocean. Spike turned and

took off toward the far end of the beach. "Where does he think he's going, Dave? There's nothing but boulders beyond here."

"I don't know, but we're not going after him. I'll stay here to keep a lookout. You go get help. Wake Brax. Call Jake. Hurry."

"You bet we're not going after him. What are you doing out here?"

"Going fishing. Didn't you read my note?"

"Didn't you listen to my voicemail?"

When he shook his head, I pressed my hands to his chest and made him promise not to do anything foolhardy. Now was not the time to explain what he'd missed. "Whatever you do, Dave, if he starts up the steps, don't confront him. There's no telling what he's capable of."

"Don't worry. If he comes this way, I'll be right behind you."

Hagrid and Christie weren't taking any chances. They hissed and herded Dave away from the steep steps as I jogged toward the inn. By now, my slippers were a muddy mess, so I kicked them off. Close by, I heard barking and a male voice calling me.

Dickens barreled into my knees as a bright light hit me. "Leta, thank goodness." It was Brax.

As I hugged Dickens, I took in Brax's explanation about Dickens waking him up, frantic to go out. "He wouldn't stop barking and pawing at the door, so I let him out. That's when I saw your cottage door standing wide open. I read the note on the counter and feared the worst, so I grabbed the flashlight and followed him. And here you are. Where's Dave? What's going on?"

"Brax, I'm not sure I know, but Dave's at the cliff and Spike's on the beach. I need to call Jake. Can you stay with Dave, please? And for goodness' sake, don't even think of chasing Spike." Without hesitation, he chased after Dickens.

Slipping and sliding across the cottage floor, I found my phone and called Jake. It was the crack of dawn, but he sounded wide awake. "DI Nancarrow."

"Jake, Spike O'Malley just tried to kill Dave, and now he's on the beach with the tide coming in. Spike, I mean, not Dave." I responded to his rapid-fire questions. "Here at the Clifftop Retreat. Yes, that beach. No, Dave's not hurt. All I know is they were going fishing, and Spike booby-trapped the path to the beach."

I put on jeans, a sweater, and wellies and started a pot of coffee before going to check on Issa.

In her robe, she was sitting in front of the fireplace. "I knew someone would come to tell me what was going on."

It wasn't for me to tell her Spike had tried to kill Dave or at the very least severely injure him. I tried to avoid out-and-out lying as I gave her an abridged version of what had transpired. "Sorry for the disturbance, Issa. Dave and Spike went fishing—not the wisest decision, given the weather. Dickens either felt left out or sensed the storm was coming in. You know how intuitive animals can be. I'm in charge of coffee."

I filled a thermos with coffee, then grabbed my parka, a flashlight, and both our phones. My thoughts swirled as I walked to the cliff. Spike had tried to kill Dave. Was I next, or Brax? How did Hagrid and Christie know something was wrong?

The last question was the only one I had any sort of answer to. Christie must have snuck out when Dave came in last night, and she and Hagrid had taken advantage of the break in the rain to wander the premises. That they discovered the tripwire was a stroke of luck.

He and Brax stood vigil at the top of the path, where Dickens had squirmed his way between them and their two feline guardian angels. Together, the three animals blocked the way. The men spoke in low voices as I approached.

When Dave spotted me, he jogged to my side. "I don't know

why you followed me out here but thank heavens you did."

I took care with my response. "It's Hagrid and Christie you need to thank." I described waking to find him gone and hearing Christie outside. "She doesn't screech for no reason, so I knew something was up."

As we joined Brax, I let him know I'd checked on Issa but hadn't given her any details.

"Thanks, Leta. She's going to take this news hard, especially after Dad." He looked at Dave. "Have you told Leta about the cats? I already explained about Dickens waking me."

"I was getting to that." He pointed at the cats, who were now nose-to-nose in matching sphinx poses. "They were lying outside when I opened the door, and they trailed after me, until I got near the steps. That's when they turned into holy terrors. Now I know what caterwauling is. Between that sound and the two of them darting between my legs, I didn't know what to think. How did they know? Because they did, didn't they?"

Shrugging, I attempted to downplay what had happened. "Either they saw Spike in action, or they spied the wire later, but they must have seen something."

He studied me. "But how did they know it was dangerous? Wouldn't they just see the wire as a plaything?" He mused aloud. "Maybe they wanted to keep it for themselves. Like when a cat brings a mouse inside or plays with a catnip toy."

I pounced on that explanation. "I bet that's it. They were afraid you'd take it away from them."

"Lucky for me, they were." He gave me a skeptical look. "And Christie was so concerned about losing her plaything, she ran to get you. There's something you're not telling me, Leta, but it can wait."

It was time to change the subject. I wanted to hear what had transpired at the pub. Then I'd get Dave to play the voicemail

I'd left him. "What happened last night? Why did Spike all of a sudden want you out of the way?"

"We're not sure, but Brax and I have an idea." I wondered whether their suppositions would line up with mine.

He ran his fingers through his hair. "Last night, we all ragged Spike about his book, and as he fetched the promised next round, Brax and I exchanged looks. We knew we were thinking the same thing—we needed to check the records again. If Spike wrote to Brax's dad as Seymour Jones, he was as likely a suspect as Dirk. In fact, given how secretive Spike was about his book, he would be at the top of the list."

I sipped my coffee. "Except Spike isn't a mind reader. How did he know what you were planning? Did you discuss it where he could overhear you?"

When Dave glanced at him, Brax took over. "We talked about that while you were gone. Our lips were zipped until we were back here. It was only as we approached Mom's cottage that we agreed we'd check the files again this morning. I doubt Spike heard us, but he must have put two and two together after yesterday."

"What about yesterday?"

"He was interviewing Mom in the sitting room while Dave and I were working in the kitchen, and he was recording their talk. We weren't loud, but we weren't making a secret of what we were doing. He must have figured out we were combing through Dad's correspondence—if not then and there, later when he played his recording."

"But he was still confident you wouldn't find anything he'd sent to him because you didn't know his pen name—or in this case, his real name."

"That's what we think. It was only after Dave showed us the book on Amazon that we learned Spike O'Malley was Seymour

Jones. What we can't figure out is why Dave and not me? I'm the one with access to Dad's records. Was Dave an opportunistic target since fishing was already on the table, and was I next on the list? And did he think you'd be a threat too?"

I blew out a big breath. "Crossed wires." That's when I had Dave play my voicemail. Their eyes widened as they listened.

Dave was the first to react. "Suicide? His sister committed suicide?"

"And Dad never minced his words about how he despised anyone who took that route," said Brax. "Who am I kidding? He never minced his words about anything."

Pulling out my phone, I clicked on the link to Spike's book. "Look at his review of *Losing Sarah*. It's ugly. Whether Spike wrote to him really doesn't matter. It's a motive."

Dave stared into the distance. "We don't need a motive for what he did here. The wire is proof enough. I wonder where he is. Hiding behind the rocks isn't going to do him much good."

The sun had come up as we stood talking, though with the clouds, it was still grey. "Dave," I said, "when is high tide? It must be close."

"Another forty-five minutes. You can see the water is already taking over the beach. If Jake doesn't get here soon, there'll be no chance of chasing Spike."

As if Dave's words had summoned him, Jake appeared, jogging down the path. Behind him came two officers. "Leta, Dave, where is he?" Dickens ran to meet him, and the cats scampered away.

As we pointed out the fishing line and the equipment on the beach, the officers stepped carefully over the trip wire and made their way down. I watched as they examined each stone step. "Clear," they both called from the bottom.

As they jogged along the rapidly disappearing beach, Dave and

Brax took turns explaining the situation to Jake. He looked at us in disbelief. "Are you telling me this all has to do with a book review?"

When he put it like that, it sounded ridiculous. But we weren't talking about just any book or just any review. Trevor Tarkington had a knack for writing stinging words, and for Spike, it had been like pouring salt in a wound. Add the comment about suicide during the panel discussion, and who knows what emotion took hold of him. Well, I guess we did know—a murderous rage. Yet neither Dave nor Dirk had sensed it while the three of them had been tossing back drinks. Odd.

The tide had already reached the cluster of boulders on the beach, and one officer was working her way behind the largest—the one where Trevor Tarkington's body had landed. In a few moments, she was back, conferring with her partner. Together, they jogged toward us.

"There's no way around. The other side is completely submerged."

Jake motioned them back to the top and questioned them when they arrived. "What do you think? Is he farther along the beach, Constable? What does it look like?"

"You can see that the cliff curves toward the sea beyond here, and the water's deeper where it juts out. It's hard to say how long it's been underwater."

Jake scowled. "Radio RNLI and head to the harbor in Port Isaac. Keep me apprised."

He must have picked up on our questioning looks. "Royal National Lifeboat Institution. They've got stations in Port Isaac and Padstow. They'll coordinate a search and rescue mission. Unless he's walked into the sea, he may have made it around The Rumps and be nearly to Port Isaac by now."

CHAPTER TWENTY-ONE

BRAX STOPPED TO CHECK on Issa and break the news to her as the rest of us walked to the main building. Jake had agreed with my suggestion of the library as the best place to await news of Spike and to fill him in more fully. When he heard every last detail about the chain of events, would he find it any more believable? I doubted it.

Until I saw the minibus pulling out of the parking lot, the trip to Tintagel hadn't entered my mind. Claire must have spotted us because the brake lights popped on. When she hopped out and headed our way, she waved to us. "DI Nancarrow, what now? Your officers said that you'd be along shortly, but I couldn't wait. I've got a tour guide lined up in Tintagel."

I couldn't catch all of the conversation, but I heard the words *fishing mishap* and marveled at the understatement. The upshot was that the minibus headed out.

When my phone pinged with a text from Wendy, I knew she wasn't buying it. "What's really going on? It doesn't take two police officers and Jake for a fishing mishap."

My reply was terse. "Top secret. Spike missing on beach. Tried to kill Dave. Search and rescue looking for him. Will keep you posted."

Spike's real name, *Losing Sarah*, and the review could wait. Nothing would be gained by Wendy and Belle sifting through every detail.

We stopped by the front desk to ask Charlie if there was a chance we could still get breakfast.

"No worries. Have a seat, and Dad will be right in to take your orders. But, DI Nancarrow, can you tell me why the police car has come and gone?"

"Charlie, I'm sorry to tell you that one of your guests was surf fishing before dawn, and he's gone missing."

She blanched. "One of my . . . you mean Spike? It can't be. He's an expert fisherman. I've got to tell Dad." As she bolted from behind the desk, Jake gave me a questioning look.

I realized he wasn't aware that Charlie knew Spike from their school days. When I explained the connection, he groaned. "Bloody hell, I could have handled that better."

George was as shaken as Charlie when he came to take our orders, and Jake apologized for how he'd delivered the news. "Please tell Charlie we've called out the RNLI. We're doing everything we can."

As George was taking our orders, Brax joined us and asked if a light breakfast could be prepared for Issa. "I'll take it to her after I'm done here so you don't have to make the trip."

Brax opened his computer. "It wasn't hard to find. Spike *did* write to Dad, though their correspondence was brief. It's funny how similar his and Dirk's emails are in tone. Dirk wasn't combative or belligerent, and neither was Spike, at least at first.

"In response to Dad calling Sienna weak, Spike provided more background on his sister's prowess in gymnastics and the multiple, painful surgeries she underwent. He detailed the procedures, the physical therapy, and the disappointing outcomes. As I read it, I imagined him thinking that once Dad knew the whole story, he'd understand why his sister didn't feel she could go on."

Brax paused as Charlie refilled our coffees and resumed when she left. "Of course, Dad wasn't persuaded, and he doubled down on what he'd written in his review. In his mind, suicide wasn't only an unacceptable choice for one person. He saw it as a slap in the face to all the children like my sister who didn't have a choice."

Closing his eyes, he shook his head. "She died when she was five years old. How could he know what she would have done in her teens, faced with the same situation as Sienna? Regardless, it's clear from Spike's last email to Dad that he was livid. In deference to Leta, I won't read it aloud."

He turned the screen around, and I winced as I read it. I'd always thought that Brits were highly creative with their expletives, and Spike's email was a perfect example. "The only thing he didn't do was outright threaten him. Still, after a message like this, I'd *feel* threatened. And if I ever met this person on the street, I'd run the other way."

"That, Leta, is because you don't thrive on conflict like my dad did. That he didn't respond to Spike tells me he was too busy at the time and forgot about it. Probably had a bigger controversy to weigh in on."

"And yet," I said, "Spike was your mom's friend. How does a relationship like that happen?"

"I haven't gone through Mom's older correspondence, but I think they were pen-pals prior to Spike's book. We'll have to ask her."

"You're right. They were. What I'm really wondering is how the friendship survived and even deepened after the emails you just showed me. Your mom told me last night Spike initially wrote to her about *Memories of Spring*, and that was before he

wrote his book." I turned to Jake. "That's how I discovered that
Spike had gotten a quintessential Snarkington review. If we'd
known that earlier, Spike would have been on our radar."

We fell silent and tried to focus on breakfast, though Jake kept
a watchful eye out for new text messages. It was a waiting game.

Charlie was refilling our mugs again when Dave spoke up.
"Charlie, Spike told me about the sea caves around here when I
told him we might go kayaking. Are there any right here, off The
Rumps?"

She went straight into innkeeper mode. "Oh yes. There's a
small one you don't want to get stuck in. We kids nicknamed it
the Worm Hole. The larger one, the Rum Cave, is big enough
to paddle into if you catch it just right. And when the tide's out,
you can walk in. The kayak tours are well worth it, but if you
want to see the cave without making a day of it, just wait for low
tide."

A shocked look appeared on her face. "Wait! Do you . . . do
you think Spike could be in one of the caves?" She checked her
smartwatch. "Low tide today is at 2:45, so it will be doable soon
after lunch if the weather holds."

Jake shot from his chair. "Bingo! Thanks, Charlie."

"Clueless old codger, indeed," said Brax. "How on earth did
you think of that?"

"Leta can tell you. It happens to her all the time. As additional
facts come to light, pieces start to fall into place. Our caving
conversation surfaced when I was running through what he and
I talked about the past few days. It seemed worth asking about,
but I bet the search and rescue teams have already thought of
it."

He looked glum. "Spike befriended me to keep an eye on you,
Leta. He knew your reputation for sleuthing, and he hoped I'd
be an entrée to your thinking. What an idiot! I even let him

see our notes in the cottage when he came over with fishing equipment."

Brax sipped his coffee. "He couldn't have been thinking straight. Taking you out of the way, temporarily or permanently, wasn't going to do the trick. Leta might have been too devastated to carry on, but not me. I would have told Jake our suspicions and, after an attempt on your life, Spike would have been the obvious suspect." I could see the wheels turning in his head. "Except he would have removed the tripwire after you fell and made out like you stumbled without any help."

Like a fly on the wall, I listened to their back-and-forth. Dave concurred. "You're right, Brax. And now that I think about it, Spike never missed an opportunity to remind me that you were the likeliest suspect. He was covering every angle. He must have felt safe until Leta dug up his book, and then, he lost the plot—so to speak."

I couldn't help groaning at that. "Seriously? You're going with a writing metaphor?"

When Brax carried breakfast to Issa, Dave followed him to grab our notes in preparation for the debrief with Jake. In no time at all, we had everything taped to the walls and were ready.

Jake held up his phone as he entered the library. "First, let me tell you that I've posted a guard at the top of the stone steps and another between The Rumps and the harbor. A search and rescue boat will meet us at one p.m. on the beach. If Spike's down there in a cave, he's not getting by us."

Sitting in a wingback chair, he took a deep breath. "Righto, let's hear it, Leta."

"It's not my story to tell. Dave's in charge."

Dave stood and took a bow. "I'm not sure I can do this justice without a laser pointer or Christie chasing it. Let's start with the original list of suspects."

At Jake's worried look, Dave chuckled. "I'm kidding, Jake. I'll cut to the chase. We eliminated Oliver early on. It wasn't scientific, but we did. The romance writers cleared me, and Brax's girlfriend finally cleared him last night. Admittedly, Leta and I had already ruled Brax out because we believed the story about his girlfriend without verifying it. It was Dirk and Spike we disagreed on. Neither had alibis. Both had written books, but only one had a contentious encounter with Trevor Tarkington that we knew of. Leta, do you have anything to add?"

"You won't like this explanation, Jake, but I just couldn't see Dirk as a killer, and I didn't know enough about Spike to make an informed call." I did, but I couldn't reveal that Hagrid had seen him with Trevor on the cliff.

Jake studied the array of notes on the wall. "Means, motive, and opportunity. Prior to the discovery of Spike O'Malley's book, you saw the emails between Dirk and Tarkington as motive, heightened by their encounter in the hallway. But Spike was still an enigma. Am I right?"

Without mentioning Hagrid, I did my best to explain my thinking. "Perhaps not for Dave, but for me, yes. I was hard-pressed to see Dirk so upset by the hallway comment that he'd wait a few hours and lure Trevor Tarkington to the cliff to push him over. And let's not forget Dirk had gone out of his way to avoid the man. I also couldn't imagine he'd sat down to drinks with him on the patio." Whether Spike lured Trevor was an unknown, but he lured Dave.

"You're back to the whiskey tumblers on the back patio, right? And you think it was Tarkington and Spike O'Malley."

"Yes. Remember the empty bottle of Macallan's? It made sense that Trevor went in search of scotch and found Spike with a bottle."

Dave winked at me. "May I continue, Tuppence? Let's fast-forward to yesterday afternoon when things heated up. Spike must have overheard Brax and me as we searched his dad's correspondence. And when I showed him his book on Amazon, he got nervous. He's a smart guy. He must have known we'd look for him in the records."

I remembered the jolt I'd felt when Spike leaned over my shoulder last night. "Dave, one more thing. Spike came up behind me before dinner as I was speaking with Wendy. I was saying I couldn't see Dirk as cold-blooded. He asked who was cold-blooded, and he may well have heard me mention Dirk. When I played it off as a discussion of our cozy mystery, he went along with my story. What if he knew I was lying?"

"The answer, Tuppence, is that the comment would have upped the ante. He knew Brax and I were actively searching for clues, and if he heard you, he knew you were too."

"If only I'd spoken to Claire earlier. Last night, I mentioned my fruitless search for Spike's book, and she told me he used his real name. I might have eventually come up with Seymour as the first name, but I never would have known that O'Malley was an invented name, too."

Jake shook his head. "But even with that info, what would have convinced you that he was the killer? It's his attempt on Dave's life that seals the deal for me. Before that, you didn't have anything more on him than you had on Dirk."

But I did. I had a witness who put him at the scene of the crime. Instead of a confidential informant, I had a CCI—confidential cat informant—and I couldn't reveal his name or his species.

A chill ran down my spine. If not for Christie and Hagrid, Dave would be dead. Worse, I knew things never would have gotten that far if Hagrid's observation had come from a human. With that information, Jake would have arrested Spike long before we dug up information on his book. Spike wouldn't have needed to do away with Dave or me or Brax.

I was hearing voices—not in a crazy sense, but arguing in my head.

I should have told Dave.

Right, and how would Dave have reacted when you told him Hagrid saw Spike?

He would have thought I was crazy.

And how would you have convinced him you weren't?

The answer was that I had no idea. I couldn't see myself doing anything other than keeping the information to myself. No one would have believed me, even the man I loved. The one thing I knew for sure was I would never have been able to forgive myself if Dave had died, knowing Hagrid's information would have saved him.

Dave's voice came as if from a distance. "Leta, are you still with us?"

"Sorry. I was playing the what if game. What if we'd known this or that sooner?"

Jake pointed to the list of motives. "You realize, don't you, that true crime never ties up neatly like it does in the movies? That the motive was revenge triggered by a mean-spirited review was a stretch for me. I planned to interview Dirk Blackthorne again and would have done the same with Spike, given the new information. But unless my impressive interview technique elicited a confession, that would have been the end of it."

"This is when I need a laser pointer," said Dave. "It's not revenge. It's loathing. Spike loathed Trevor Tarkington. He may not have been as drunk as I was, but he was drunk enough to let Tarkington get under his skin. Whether it was the suicide comment during the panel discussion or another vile remark from Tarkington, Spike's composure unraveled. Maybe it was a combination."

I sat forward. "Here's another piece of the puzzle. As calm as Spike's been, I don't think he came here planning to kill Tarkington. I learned last night that Issa and Spike are incredibly close, so there's no way this was a premeditated murder. He wouldn't have done that to her."

"And," said Jake, "he panicked. I wonder if he realizes he'd be home free if not for his stupidity this morning."

I wonder whether he's still alive.

CHAPTER TWENTY-TWO

Jake spent the next half hour walking around the room and scribbling notes on the pages taped to the wall. When he was done, he took photos, and rolled up the pages to take with him. "I'm amazed you two don't travel with a whiteboard."

Dave glanced at me with a grin. "Leta, do you think Cynthia could find us one?" Cynthia was the interior designer who had furnished Dave's he-shed in our garden. She'd cleverly turned one side of an antique wooden screen into a whiteboard.

A subdued Charlie interrupted his description of his he-shed when she poked her head in the door at noon to ask about lunch. Sure that we would need fortification for the upcoming beach search, we eagerly accepted.

I stopped Jake before we exited the library. "How much did you tell her about the police cars, Jake? Just that Spike was missing?"

"Since she figured it out when I mentioned a fisherman, yes, I told her Spike was fishing on the beach and had disappeared. She didn't need to know about the fishing line."

"Would it make sense to let her guide us to the Rum Cave? You'd need to tell her the whole story, though, wouldn't you?"

"If not Charlie, her dad. I'll take care of that now. Keep on like this, Leta, and I'll be asking you to relocate to Cornwall." I suspected his girlfriend Gemma would be delighted with that prospect. She didn't appreciate my so-called help anywhere near as much as he did.

I'd texted Brax earlier about meeting at one, and he was standing with the guard at the top of the stone steps. Gone was the fishing line across the steps. Jake had taken photos from every angle and bagged it. Now the path was only treacherous because it was slick from the rain.

The guard pointed toward Port Isaac. "There's the RIB. They set out fifteen minutes ago from the harbor."

At my confused look, Brax explained. "I've gotten an education, Leta. I immediately thought of tasty ribs with sauce, but a RIB is a rigid inflatable boat. They're designed for rapid response and are especially effective for search and rescue operations close to shore."

George, who had insisted he be the one to accompany us, elaborated. "That's right. And if they can't float into the cave, they can get close enough to shore to deploy equipment."

By the time we gingerly made our way down the steps, the RIB was stationed past the large clump of boulders. Jake jogged over with Brax and Dave on his heels. George and I were slower. Two burly, bearded men leaped ashore, and a third man handed them what looked like a spotlight.

I arrived in time to hear the decision about the approach. The man with the red beard pointed toward his partner. "Robbo here will go in first. He says Rum Cave is deep and wide, but it narrows as it goes back, and it partially floods at high tide. We'll know soon enough whether anyone's holed up in there. Now, do I understand you consider the bloke dangerous?"

"It's best to assume he is, and that means I'm going in with Robbo." Now I knew why Jake had donned his safety vest. I shuddered at the image of Spike, possibly armed with a fishing knife.

When Dave made to follow them, Jake stopped him. "No way, Dave. He's probably cold, wet, and weak, but I'm not taking any chances."

The entrance to the cave was six feet above the beach and set back with an overhang. If I hadn't known it was there, I would have taken it for a shadow on the cliff face. The two bearded men were more sure-footed than Jake as they leaped from rock to rock to make their way to the cave, but eventually all three stood at the entrance.

The words *Spike O'Malley* echoed from the cave and faded as they went deeper. If they hadn't found him in the water, did that mean he was in a cave? Or had he moved fast enough to get to Port Isaac and hide out somewhere? Or had he drowned trying to escape?

George pointed toward Port Isaac. "If he's not in there, I'll show you the Wormhole. It's tucked a tad farther along the cliff and harder to see. But since he grew up here, my money's on the Rum Cave. Probably took my daughter in there—the older one."

It seemed like forever before Robbo emerged from the cave with a shout. "He's here. We need a stretcher."

Dave moved fast. He waded to the boat, grabbed the stretcher held out to him, and clambered over the rocks. Robbo motioned him to remain at the cave entrance as he took the stretcher inside. When he and his partner appeared with Spike between them, a hand lifted from the stretcher and motioned toward Dave.

After a nod from Jake, Dave leaned over and turned his ear to Spike. He grasped Spike's hand before stepping back. As the rescue team made its way to the RIB, Dave and Jake hung back. My assumption was that Dave was telling Jake what Spike had said.

The decision was made to take Spike to the Royal Cornwall Hospital in Truro, as it offered extensive emergency care capabilities. Only after the RIB departed did I ask Dave what Spike said to him.

He looked at his hand as if in disbelief. "I couldn't catch every word, but it was an apology of sorts. Something like, 'It wasn't about you, mate. It got away from me. Sorry.' You'd think he'd merely tossed a drink in my face, not that he'd tried to kill me." He shook himself. "I shouldn't, but I almost feel sorry for him."

Jake accompanied us back to the parking lot after dismissing the guard. "Spike's bruised and battered, but according to Robbo, his worst injuries are broken ribs and a sprained wrist. He could have internal bleeding as well, so we're not taking any chances. I'll be waiting in A&E so I can speak with him as soon as the doctors let me." He promised to keep us posted.

Feeling near tears, I tugged Dave toward our cottage. "I'm ready for some time alone, just the two of us."

"You'll get no argument from me. I'm worn out."

Christie barely stirred when I plopped down on the couch. It was only when Dave joined me with two cups of tea that she squirmed her way between us. When she stood to lick the tears from my face, Dave took a good look at me. "Aww, sweetheart.

It's been a rough day, hasn't it?"

"Now I know how you felt all those times someone came after me. It doesn't matter that I never set out to put myself in danger."

Shushing me, he held me close. "If only I'd listened to your voicemail, I would have been on the alert. Would I have gone to meet Spike regardless? I'm not sure. It was a close call, but thanks to you and Christie, I'm fine."

Christie tapped his face with her paw. "Don't forget Hagrid. He saw the earring man by the steps."

"Dave, that would have been intentionally putting yourself in danger. Please tell me you wouldn't have done that."

"You're right, Leta. I might have risked it this morning, but I've learned an important lesson. It's time we were both more cautious."

Hearing the minibus motor, I groaned. "I can't face Wendy and Belle right now, much less a class on Point of View. I feel like a truck hit me."

He kissed the top of my head. "Why don't you take a nap? I'll intercept them and bring them up to speed. After all, you put me in charge of this investigation."

When my Billy Joel ringtone woke me, I couldn't believe it was six o'clock.

"Rise and shine, sleepyhead. I texted you twice, but when you didn't answer, I knew you were dead to the world. Are you ready to face cocktails and dinner?"

"Dinner, yes. Cocktails, no. A fluff and dust won't do this time. I need a shower. Save me a seat, please."

As I opened the door, Christie darted out. "You're becoming quite the night owl, aren't you?"

"Hagrid makes it fun. First, we get treats from Chef Duncan. Then we find a lap to snuggle in. And best of all, we explore. You can't believe the treasures we find."

I made it to dinner as everyone was taking their seats. The LOLs had the table by the window, and Dave stood to pull out my chair. "You look like a new person, Tuppence. Wine?"

In reply, I held up my wineglass. "If that's true, I shudder to think what I looked like before my nap. Wine should help."

"You owe me, Leta. I had to give Wendy and Belle every last detail of today's happenings to keep them from calling you. I'm sure they'll have to hear it from you all over again, but perhaps not tonight." He gave our sleuthing partners a meaningful look.

Wendy raised her glass but kept her voice down. "A toast to smart sleuths, to strange cats, and to surviving unscathed."

As we clinked our glasses, Belle's eyes gleamed. "I found a gift for Christie in Tintagel. Had I known she was going to save Dave, I would have gotten her treats too."

Dave winked. "That's a grand idea, Belle. To show my gratitude, I may have to lay in a supply of special treats for her."

Issa had understandably bowed out of the Point of View session, so Claire had postponed it to the next day and would spend the evening boning up on the topic. According to Wendy, most of the group had used the extra time to write and rest. She'd taken copious notes at Tintagel in anticipation of a cozy mystery based on our first trip there. "You know, Leta, we already have a ready-made plot, but bringing the setting to life will be equally important."

Tilting his head, Dave studied her. "As I recall, the investigation involved a pub crawl, or at least that's how you two described it to me."

As a euphemism for our real mission that night, it wasn't half bad. It was yet another instance when we hadn't intentionally put ourselves in harm's way, but things had gone awry. Rather than comment, I took a bite of the sticky toffee pudding Chef Duncan had prepared for dessert.

I was looking forward to an early night when Dave said, "I didn't expect to see you tonight."

It was Jake. "It could have waited, but I know the celebratory dinner is tomorrow night, and I thought I would give the group time to adjust to the news before then. And, honestly, I'd rather wrap up this part. I've still got all kinds of paperwork to tend to. Let me speak to Claire, and I'll make this short."

As George cleared the tables, Jake motioned Claire to the hallway. I wasn't sure how much he told her, but she was pale when she returned. All it took was for Jake to stand in the doorway for the voices to die down.

"I want to thank you for your cooperation and patience these past few days. To say it's been a difficult time would be an understatement, and I sincerely hope tonight's update will put your minds at ease. Still, it won't be easy news to digest.

"What I'm about to tell you has already been shared with Issa and Brax Tarkington. First, we have arrested Spike O'Malley in connection with the death of Trevor Tarkington. Whether the charge will be manslaughter or murder has yet to be determined."

Jake waited for the gasps to die down and ignored the questions about what had happened on the cliff. "In addition, early this morning, Mr. O'Malley allegedly made an attempt on the life of Dave Prentiss. Again, whether the charge will be attempted murder or grievous bodily harm with intent remains to be seen."

Allegedly, my foot. He was safely on the beach, and the wire was in place. Unless he had a partner, there was no question it was him.

The room erupted in questions, but Jake refused to be drawn in and repeated several times that the Crown Prosecution Service would review the evidence and determine what charges to bring in both situations. I could only hope he'd be more forthcoming with the LOLs.

"Now, if you'll excuse me, I need to speak with Mr. Prentiss and be on my way." He motioned to Dave and didn't object when I accompanied him. The three of us slipped into the library, where Jake shared several key pieces of information.

"Spike wanted me to tell you this, Dave, but I'd prefer you didn't share it. If he's telling the truth, he didn't intend to kill Tarkington. They started drinking on the patio and continued on the clifftop. If Spike's sister hadn't come up, Tarkington would still be alive today."

Dave grasped my hand. "His sister? How on earth....?"

"How did it come up? Spike wasn't clear about that, but it did. And this time, Tarkington compared her to Oscar Pistorius. It doesn't excuse Spike's actions, but can you imagine someone comparing your sister—unfavorably—to a man who killed his girlfriend?"

I gasped. "You mean the Blade Runner, the one with the prosthetic legs? He compared Sienna to the Blade Runner? How could he?"

"Who knows? Apparently, when he praised the man's bravery and fortitude as compared to Sienna's giving up, Spike lost it. He claims he barely remembers shoving him, and it was all over in a flash."

Dave stiffened. "And me? What did he have to say about me?"

"He couldn't say he flew off the handle, that's for sure. He blathered about being cornered and desperate, but he didn't confess to doing it. I'm confident the forensics will show he strung the wire, and that will be that. Whether he intended to kill you or merely injure you may be more difficult to discern, but it doesn't matter. Both attempted murder and grievous bodily harm carry lengthy sentences."

I grasped Dave's hand. "What matters is that you're still alive."

We left the library hand in hand. "Leta, I'm sure Belle and Wendy expect an update, and the others are no doubt hoping to hear what happened this morning. Are you up for that?" When I mouthed a no, he gave me a hug and said he'd handle it. I was in no mood to revisit any of it.

Standing on the back patio, I wondered why I felt so weepy. *Admit it*, I told myself. *It's guilt. You can't get over the fact that you could have prevented the attempt on Dave's life if only you'd somehow shared Hagrid's eyewitness account.*

The if onlys and what ifs were driving me crazy. I walked toward the cliff and retraced the path I'd taken several times that day. Sitting on the bench, I stared into the distance and argued with myself. *Do I or don't I?* It was a risky step. If I chose to do it, I'd have to find the perfect opportunity, and there'd be no going back.

CHAPTER TWENTY-THREE

WENDY JOINED US AT the window table for breakfast. "You two are looking chipper this morning. No dawn derring-do today?"

"Bite your tongue," I said. "If there's even a hint of adventure today, it will be on the page, not in real life. I may—'may' being the operative word—write a paragraph or two, but that's it."

"If you have anything new written, you could join this afternoon's critique group. That will help get you back in the swing of things. And then there's the send-off dinner. I can't wait to see what Chef Duncan serves for that."

"We'll see. Where's your mum today?"

"Would you believe Brax is taking Issa and Mum to Port Isaac? He's doing everything he can to distract his mother, and Mum's delighted at the prospect of a return trip. He's hired a tour guide who's mapped out a short, doable route for Issa's wheelchair, which means it will also be doable for Mum with her cane. The highlight is a boat tour of the harbor."

Dave and I agreed that the patio behind our cottage was as far as we planned to venture today. "Tell you what, Leta, I'll grab Dickens and take a leisurely run while you're at the Point of View Palooza. Then we can kick back and relax until dinner."

In the library, I purposely chose a chair at the far end of the first row with Wendy by my side. Hopefully, that would discourage our fellow writers from badgering me for additional details about the day before.

My ploy worked. When Dirk chose the chair behind me, he leaned over and whispered, "Glad to see you," and left it at that. Claire gave me a similar greeting before taking a seat behind the desk.

She spent most of the session on first and third person, the most common POVs in fiction writing. When she referenced *The Virgin Suicides* as an example of fourth person, my ears perked up. How odd to hear that title several times in one week. I didn't recall the story being told from the perspective of a group of teenage boys, but its connection to Trevor Tarkington was something I would never forget.

Other than lunch with the group, Dave and I spent the rest of the day at our cottage. I attempted to write, but the words wouldn't come, so I gave myself permission to procrastinate. That decision allowed me to skip the critique session, too.

When I mentioned feeling like a slacker, Dave told me to get a grip. "You could use a day with no pressure. Why don't you do something fun, like mapping out the wedding venues you want to see over the next few days?"

"That's a grand idea. I have a few places on the list, but I'm sure there are others."

"Did I tell you about Jake's cousins? He says they have a farm in Truro with rental cottages and an old barn they've outfitted for events."

"No! We'll have to check it out. I'm torn between formal and informal—an historic church or castle or something rustic." I happily spent the rest of the day Googling wedding venues and dozing.

Showering and dressing for dinner with plenty of time to spare was nice for a change. I'd packed my favorite red dress and black boots for what Claire deemed an elegantly relaxed dinner.

Dave was in his usual position, propped up on the bed, watching as I put on my jewelry and spritzed Shalimar above my head. As I turned to face him, he swung his legs off the bed. "The spritz! That's the signal that you're ready to go."

Dinner tray in hand, Brax was opening the door to Willow Cottage. "Good evening. Mom's worn out after her Port Isaac tour, so she'll be eating in tonight. I'll see you guys in a few minutes."

The bar was set up in the front room again, and the atmosphere, if not jovial, was not as somber as it had been the past few evenings. Only Charlie still seemed subdued. It had to be hard to discover that your sister's onetime boyfriend had killed one man and tried to do in another.

George was moving through the room with a tray of appetizers. When he approached us, he described the smoked mackerel pâté and Cornish pasty bites as Chef Duncan's appetizer specialties. "He created these for the Coastal Kitchen, and they've been a big hit."

"They're too exquisite," exclaimed Nora as she came our way with Evie. "And I love that red dress, Leta."

"Thank you. It's an oldie but a goodie."

Dave's eyes twinkled. "She was wearing it the night we met. Will you put that detail in your later-in-life romance?"

Giving Nora a nudge, Evie cautioned us. "Watch what you say. She's already outlined a new book loosely based on your story. The names, of course, will be changed to protect the innocent."

Behind us, Wendy chimed in. "Oh my. Will the woman be an amateur sleuth like Leta?"

Nora shook her head. "No. Pure romance. I'm not a mystery

writer."

When Oliver and Dirk walked up, the conversation turned to the critique group meeting. Dirk wasn't leaving his latest thriller behind but had temporarily shifted gears to the opening of another historical fiction novel. "With Claire's encouragement, that will be my next project. The material in Gran's journal will give me enough background to flesh out a second female resistance fighter."

Dave and I joined Brax and Claire for dinner, and we chose a bottle of red for the table. A Roasted Beetroot and Goat Cheese Salad was the first course. Chef Duncan was going all out tonight, and we all agreed he'd outdone himself thus far.

"Claire," said Brax, "I've only been on the periphery this week, but it seems like the workshop has gone well, despite . . . you know."

"Thank you, Brax. Yes, I wasn't sure we could pull it off, but the writers maintained their focus, and I think they accomplished their goals. Your mother certainly set the example by rallying to teach a session and provide the one-on-one coaching. I still can't believe she did that."

I raised my glass. "Here's to Issa Wright, an amazing woman in so many ways."

"That she is. Thank you. We've gotten word we can take Dad home midweek, and she's relieved about that. Now, we can plan the memorial service, and she'll rest better at home." He glanced at Dave. "By the way, she asked if you could stop by tonight, Dave. She has something she'd like to discuss with you."

"Sure thing. I don't see Leta and me making a late night of it. We're setting out early to visit wedding venues."

That comment led to a discussion of Claire's wedding plans. She'd found a dress, but she and Simon hadn't set a date yet. "I know people think the publishing business is seasonal, and it is, but we're always busy."

After a scrumptious main course of Cornish Lamb Shank, I wanted to skip dessert, but the description of the Lemon Posset did away with that idea. A lemon cream dessert with shortbread biscuits sounded divine.

When Chef Duncan opened the kitchen door, he got a round of applause. Claire stood as the clapping died down. "Thank you, Chef Duncan. I knew the food would be good, but you've far exceeded my expectations. I may have to make a special trip to Padstow when I next visit Cornwall."

She picked up her glass. "And to my guests. What an astonishing group you've been. And I'm talking about much more than writing. Not one of you questioned the idea of continuing the workshop, and you gave it your all. Hear, hear!"

Telling my tablemates I'd see them at breakfast, I excused myself. I'd had a restful day, but try as I might, I hadn't shaken off the emotional hangover I had from the day before.

I looked around for Christie, but she was nowhere to be seen. No doubt she was out gallivanting on her last night with Hagrid. Either that, or she was waiting for treats from Chef Duncan. Dickens was still with Issa, so I had the cottage to myself. Perhaps he'd come home with Dave. If not, he'd be with us for sure tomorrow.

Staring into the fire, I considered my conundrum. I knew if I waited long enough, the sense of urgency would pass. I'd tell myself it really hadn't been a big deal, and I'd let it go. Until the next time. *And then what? Do I or don't I?*

An hour later, Dave walked in with a bottle of cabernet. "Look who I've got, both Dickens and Christie. And look at you, still awake."

Dickens pranced in front of me, demanding attention. He yipped and put his paws in my lap. "I miss you, Leta. Can I stay now?"

"Leta, if we can get Dickens to calm down, how about a glass of wine?"

As Dave uncorked the bottle, Dickens prattled on. By the time Dave handed me my glass, Dickens was sitting with his head on my knee, and Christie had taken up position on the arm of the couch. "Finally, the whole family together again."

"And what a perfect family it is." He swirled the wine in his glass and took a small sip. "What do you think?"

I savored my first taste. "Oh, I like this. Dickens tells me that Brax gave you the bottle."

His glass was halfway to his lips when he stopped. "What did you say?"

"Dickens says Brax gave you the bottle."

"Funny, Leta. What else does Dickens say?"

"Hold on." I tapped Dickens's nose. "Dickens, what was the other thing you told me?"

When he yipped softly, I chuckled. "No, silly boy, you can't go unless you want to ride in a cargo hold again." He hadn't liked the nine-hour trip to England in his crate.

Scooting to the end of the couch, I turned to face Dave. "Something about a trip to Boston. He wants to go with us."

The grin on his face seemed forced. "Is this some kind of elaborate joke?"

"Trust me, it's not. I have something I need to tell you." I took a deep breath. "Dickens and Christie talk to me."

"I know that. They talk to everyone."

"But I understand what they say."

"What does that mean?"

"When I tell you that Christie wants her food fluffed and that Dickens wants to see the donkeys, it's because they told me."

His eyes widened, and he took a gulp of wine. "What's this all about, Leta? You haven't been yourself since . . . since you . . ."

"Since I showed up at the cliff with Christie?"

"Yes. I know it was a close call, but it's over now. Everything's fine. Isn't it?"

Moving closer to him, I sat my glass down and did the same with his. I brought up the conversation on the cliff about the cats thinking the fishing line was a toy. "When I agreed with you, you said, 'there's something you're not telling me.' Do you remember that?"

It took a moment, but he finally gave me a hesitant nod.

"There was, Dave. There was." Grasping his hands, I recounted my story. How I'd been able to talk to the animals since I was a child. How I'd kept it hidden my whole life—until now.

He blinked and chewed his lower lip. "You're telling me that you talk to the animals, like Doctor Dolittle?"

From her position on the couch arm, Christie meowed and pawed his elbow. "Who's that?"

"And if I'm to believe you, Christie just said something you understood?"

She meowed again. "Enough of that. Tell him he left my new toy behind by the big fireplace. Belle gave me a fat little bird. It has feathers."

"Yes. I know you think I'm pulling your leg, or worse, you think I'm crazy. But she says Belle gave her a toy with feathers—a fat bird, to be exact."

He studied my face. "O—kay. This sounds serious."

"It is, and I know what you're thinking. Belle must have told me about the toy, right? And somehow, I found out about

Boston, but not from Dickens. You think Brax told me at dinner. Because you don't believe me."

"I want to believe you. It would explain a lot, but . . . I always thought you were just very attached to Dickens and Christie. And talked to them the way other people talk to their animals. This is a lot to take in, Leta."

I whispered. "I knew this was a mistake. I knew you wouldn't believe me."

He shifted me around and pulled me into his arms. "It's been an emotional few days, sweetheart. Shall we pick this up in the morning?"

Pulling myself from his arms, I stood in front of the couch. "No! We're not going to bed with you thinking I'm crazy. I'm going to try one more thing to prove to you that I'm telling the truth. I want you to take Dickens and Christie outside. Go as far away as you think necessary to ensure I can't hear you. Go to the cliff if you must. Tell them something I couldn't possibly know. Something you've never told me. Something I couldn't have overheard or read."

Stammering, he got to his feet. "And if you can tell me what I said, I'll have to believe you. But, Leta, if you don't, what happens then?"

I pursed my lips. "We'll cross that bridge *if* we come to it."

As I berated myself for the stupid idea of telling Dave my secret, I washed my face and threw on my gown and robe. If nothing else, I would show him I hadn't left the cottage. I hadn't snuck out to follow him so I could eavesdrop on his conversation with Dickens and Christie. *He has to believe me.* When one of my favorite songs flashed into my brain, I pulled it up on my phone. If "A Matter of Trust" wasn't apropos, I didn't know what was.

I was listening to the song for the umpteenth time when he walked in the door with Christie squirming in his arms and

Dickens at his heels. Christie leaped down and darted to the bedroom. Dickens stood by the fire.

Dave hesitated by the door, crossing and uncrossing his arms. It seemed like an eternity before he came around the kitchen counter and embraced me. "I love you, Leta Parker, no matter what."

It was now or never. If need be, I'd get Christie to join us, but for now, I would depend on Dickens. I called him to my side. "Dickens, what did Dave tell you?"

"He said it was a secret." I wanted to laugh, but the situation was much too serious.

"Dave, would you please tell him he can share the secret?"

Leaning over, he lifted Dickens's chin. "You can tell her, boy." His eyes darted to me with a questioning look as he stood.

Dickens put his paws on my thighs. "It's funny, Leta. He says his name was Froggy when he was little. He doesn't look like a frog to me."

I laughed in relief. "Froggy? Seriously, you were called Froggy? The character in the *Little Rascals*?"

Watching the emotions play across Dave's face was like seeing a film. Shock and disbelief warred with relief. When he laughed and lifted me off my feet, I knew relief had won out. "How could I have doubted you? My very own Doctor Dolittle!"

"When you said we were a perfect family, did you ever imagine this?"

He pulled me to the couch. "No, never. But how can I be the only one who knows? You told Henry, right?"

"I've never told a soul. Henry and I both worked demanding jobs and weren't together day in and day out. That may be why it was easier to keep it a secret. Like you, he thought it was charming the way I seemed to converse with our animals. But you and me? We're together all the time. I kept finding myself having to be careful not to let on, and things came to a head this week."

"How?"

I explained about Hagrid seeing Spike at the cliff with Trevor. How I couldn't figure out a way to tell anyone, and how guilty I felt.

"Hold on. That's a lot to unpack. First, do you understand all the animals?"

"No. Thank goodness. I'd never have a moment's peace if I did. I understand dogs and cats. That's it. Not Martha and Dylan or the birds or other creatures."

"That means you understand Basil and Paddington and every cat and dog we meet. Fascinating. Now, let me think. Hagrid saw Spike with Trevor, but he didn't see the struggle, right? He doesn't know how Trevor went over."

"Right, but it was still a clue I couldn't reveal. I couldn't say that I saw them or that another person saw them. Can you imagine me telling Jake that a cat was my eyewitness?"

"Based on my unfortunate reaction to your strange talent, yes, I can. It wouldn't have been pretty. But let's get one thing straight. There's no need for you to feel guilty. You said yourself, Jake still wouldn't have had enough to arrest Spike."

"But he would have at least questioned him again. And Spike would have known that removing you from the picture wouldn't help one iota. If only I could have figured it out."

Instead of responding to my comment, he stood and put another log in the wood-burning stove. He had to be overwhelmed with everything I'd thrown at him.

"Here's what I know. You've given me lots to think about, and I have tons of questions, but I know one thing for sure. You have no reason to feel guilty about anything. So, can you put that out of your mind, please?"

He took a deep breath. "Beyond that, I'm both excited and apprehensive. As in, what if I mess up and let the cat out of the bag? No offense to Christie. Can I learn to understand them too? Do you think they can learn hand or paw language?"

I burst out laughing. "Paw language! I'm sure they can. Just remember that Christie's a cat, and a sassy one, to boot. Dickens will be eager to do whatever makes you happy, and Christie will decide whether she cares enough to bother."

"Right. She's a princess. How could I forget? But seriously, it's like I'm embarking on my very own magical mystery tour with you and Dickens and Christie. I'm over-the-top wowed!"

Winking at him, I joked. "You're wowed? How do you think I feel finding out I have a fiancé whose nickname is Froggy?"

He waggled his finger at me. "Hey, that's still a secret. I was the only kid in my class with glasses. And it wasn't until I started running track that my parents finally agreed to let me get contacts. And then came laser surgery, thank goodness."

"And Boston. Do you want to tell me about that? Or shall I ask Dickens?"

"I can't believe that slipped my mind. Well, actually I can. Issa wanted to see me for two reasons. One, to say how sorry she was that our involvement in the investigation put me in danger and, at the same time, to thank me for figuring it out. Of course, I told her it was you, not me."

"How can she be so strong? Trust me, in her position, concern for you would have been the last thing on my mind. Finding out Spike killed her husband had to be a major blow. You should have heard how she spoke about Spike. In different ways, she lost a husband and a friend this week."

"I know. She looked frail, but her voice was strong, and she wanted to talk business. You won't believe this, but she asked me to write the article, 'Spotlight on Issa Wright.' Spike was doing it freelance, and she felt it would be easy for me to step in and complete it. And she agreed we'd start from the beginning. I may see if Jake can get me the recording from Spike's phone, so I'm not starting from scratch."

"That's great news, Dave. Do you have time in your schedule?"

"I'll make the time. And that's where the trip to Boston comes in. We're both invited to see the author in her element. If we visit the States for Thanksgiving or Christmas, she said we could make that work. If not, we'll shoot for early next year. By the way, I heard you tell Dickens he couldn't go."

"All he had to hear was cargo hold, and he was fine with staying behind."

He pulled me off the couch. "Lots and lots to absorb, and I have tons of questions, but we need to get an early start in the morning. Shall we call it a night? I'm too excited to sleep, but we can't stay up all night talking."

I put my lips to his ear. "Perhaps we can come up with another option."

I woke the next morning to Dave whispering in my ear. "I didn't dream it, did I?"

"No. It wasn't a dream." I rolled over and propped myself up on one elbow. "What are you thinking?"

"That you're nothing short of amazing. What other surprises do you have in store for me?"

"Nothing of that magnitude. Trust me."

"I still can't believe it—no, I don't mean it that way! I believe you, and I feel like . . . like marrying you gives a completely different meaning to the words 'starting a new life together.' I don't know how to describe it."

He touched my cheek. "And how do you feel?"

"Much the way you described last night—excited, apprehensive. It sounds anticlimactic, but I'm relieved. I worked so hard to keep my strange little quirk a secret that I never dreamed of my life being any different. Until I told you, I didn't realize there was a small piece of me missing. Being able to share it with you is that piece—oh my goodness, is it too hokey to say I feel complete?"

Rolling me over, he kissed me. "Never."

We lay there for a moment, each with our separate thoughts, until we heard Dickens's tail thumping by the bed. Christie must have taken that as her signal to leap on the bed and greet us.

Dave scratched her head. "Way to ruin a romantic moment, princess."

Wedging her way between us, she meowed. "It's time for breakfast."

"Let me guess, she wants food. I don't have to understand the words to know that. And what does Dickens have to say?"

When Dickens barked, "I say let's go," I laughed and translated for Dave.

Both animals bounded from the room as he put his feet on the floor. "I'll tend to the menagerie, and then we'll get on the road."

He leaned over the bed and kissed me. "Let the magical mystery tour begin."

The End

Book XII

A delightful vacation. An astonishing dispatchment. Will Leta uncover why the victim was fatally retired?

Arriving at a luxurious Cotswold estate with her friends for a winter retreat, she's happily scouting for a wedding venue. But the peaceful trip takes a shocking turn when a dead body is discovered. Can she steer through a blizzard of suspicion to solve the case? Read *Paintings, Puppies & Murder* to find out.

What was Leta's life like before she retired to the Cotswolds? How did Dickens & Christie become part of the family?

Find out in *Paws, Claws & Mischief*—the prequel to the Dickens & Christie mystery series. Join my newsletter today to gain special access to a subscribers-only area on my website. Get behind-the-scenes exclusives, recipes from my books, your complimentary copy of the prequel, and so much more. New content awaits you every month—don't miss out!

Would you like to help others discover the world of Dickens & Christie? If so, please leave an honest review on Amazon, Goodreads, and/or BookBub. Readers depend on reviews to help them decide what to read next. It doesn't have to be a book report! A short I loved it is all it takes.

About the Author

THE OLDEST OF THREE girls, Kathy Manos Penn was the shy bookworm in a boisterous New York City family of Greeks and Italians. She took a book everywhere she went—to family dinners, doctors' offices, and, of course, to bed. A lifelong word nerd and grammar geek, she freely admits she's addicted to playing *Words with Friends* and to reading.

She populates her mysteries with well-read, witty senior women, a sassy cat, and a loyal dog. Book One in her Dickens & Christie series won a Readers' Favorite Gold Medal Award, and Kathy was nominated for a 2023 Georgia Author of the Year award.

"Never in my wildest dreams did I see myself writing cozy mysteries," she says. But somehow, after years in banking, that's what happened. Now, happily retired, she lives in Georgia with her husband and the two four-legged office assistants who inspire the personalities of Dickens & Christie.